Pursuing Fedhisss

An outer space odyssey

By

William A. Glasser

Published by Open Books

Copyright © 2020 by William A. Glasser

Interior design by Siva Ram Maganti

Cover image "Children's illustration UFO in the starry sky. Icon, silhouette in the linear style" © rodnikovay shutterstock. com/g/rodnikovay

ISBN-13: 978-1948598347

1.

THE SPACE VESSEL APPROACHING the outer fringes of earth's atmosphere was peculiarly small, an ovoid form with a transparent dome at the narrow top. It was arcing downward toward the twilight rim of the planet, as if in a slow free-fall out of the loneliness of space.

The darkened area under the dome, structured for no more than a single occupant, appeared to be empty. As the vessel made its way into the atmosphere, a circle of control panels around the inner edge of the dome brightened, filling the dome with light, and the outer surface of the vessel suddenly became sensory.

The density of earth's atmosphere was felt now, all the elements of upper air to the least traces, and a fluctuating variety of electrical impulses, natural and artificial. The space vessel moved through them, touching and sorting, accepting everything into itself. Continuing downward, it gathered in a welter of communicating waves and pulses that intensified around the descending vessel, as though earth itself, responding to the vessel's arrival, had become confusedly, radiantly alive.

Six miles above the surface of the planet, in dusky twilight, the space vessel stopped its descent. It hovered, motionless, for ninety seconds, scanning all areas contained now within the encircling horizon. It descended then to one mile and paused again as it sensed the contours of the land directly below—an extensively wooded area on the outskirts of a small town.

At an adjusted angle of two degrees, the vessel suddenly streaked down from its height into a section of the woods, passing the treetops with the speed of an imminent crash until, with a startling brake in its descent, it simply stopped—precisely at the moment it made contact with the ground.

Settled now among the interweaving branches of trees and underbrush in the thickly growing woods, the small vessel could barely be seen. Its lighted dome, casting a soft radiance onto the nearby leaves, was still empty inside.

Beneath the vessel, two metallic probes suddenly penetrated the ground. The tips of the probes, like powerful magnets, began to attract a rush of molecules out of the rich humus of the earth. Elemental materials that were sensed now as the multitudinous leavings of life, thousands upon thousands of crumbled life forms composing the fertile soil, were being taken into the vessel by the probes until, within the lighted dome of the vessel, a shape slowly began to appear.

2.

...I AM SUBMITTING...AS A formal record of my visit...an account of the brief time i will have existed on this unfortunate planet.... the report...to be filed in our archives for future study...will be cast in one of the indigenous languages of the dominant inhabitants...which can be expressed in visual representations of units of sound.... it will be a new experience for me to manipulate such a rudimentary means of conveying the contents of consciousness....

...although I remain uncertain at this point...i am considering the questionable decision of whether to awaken the inhabitants to the underlying dire nature of their existence... of which they remain apparently...and so all the more remarkably...ignorant....

...advancing their awareness will of course require a superhuman effort [i do appreciate their sense of humor].... however...having experienced the workings of a human body and its contained mind...and having noted the tenacity with which they cling to their present state of ignorance...i declare here for the record that i do not believe i will succeed....

...it is evident that they will initially be concerned to the point of distraction about my own nature and background... my point of origin... destination...the purpose of my visit... how i am able to communicate with them in their own language...and a mess of other mysteries [i also like the sensuous weightings of their words].... i begin my account therefore by responding to that need in one of their more practiced forms...with the intention of gathering for our archives a few representative samplings from the variety of their other forms as I proceed ... .and so I begin with the following ....

Continuing my pursuit, I entered a previously unexplored sector, which includes a system of nine bodies orbiting a minor star at the edge of a spiral arm in a secondary galaxy. After scanning the system for signs of life, my vehicle landed on the third body, entering what would prove to be a new and troublesome phase in our awareness of other forms of life.

Judging solely from my own direct experiences, and after considering the successful completion of my two earlier exploratory landings, I can report that my vehicle need no longer to be categorized as experimental, since it has performed up to all expectations. The vehicle's capacity to contain my presence in unmattered energy units across the far reaches of space has now been proven three-fold, as has its ability to re-infuse that energy into various gatherings of matter to occupy new and different life forms.

The currently dominant inhabitants of this planet, by the time of my arrival, had developed the means to communicate in electronic pulses. There were varied kinds of basic information pervading the atmosphere upon my entry and accessible to my vehicle's detection, including visual representations of the inhabitants, their activities, and their fabricated settings. Since the vehicle's program for my energy infusion also included these materials, I was awakened to the realization that I had been given both the physical mobility and the basic information needed to survive my visit to this planet. However, I was awakened to another realization that startled me beyond belief.

I stress here for the record the danger that we recognized would accompany energy infusion. The nature of the life form into which we are placed and subsequently awakened by this process obviously is not a matter of preference. It is determined by the life forms already existing on the planet at the time of the visit. Before we so dramatically extended our means of exploration through the development of energy infusion, we had categorized twenty-three basic structures and seventeen developmental levels of life within our known region. These discoveries revealed nothing that would cause us to be seriously concerned, nor did the life forms found on the last two planets I visited. But we must recognize now, and appropriately respond to, the existence of a different life form, for on this planet I was awakened within a body and its contained mind that has the capacity to destroy another of its own kind. And of even greater surprise, along with an unexpected dread, is the fact that this is not an aberrant behavior here. All life forms on this astonishing planet are destroying other life forms.

So the pertinent question now is…Why?

Still caught within the uncontrolled evolutionary swirlings of matter, the various life forms currently existing here remain unstable and rudimentary. Only the dominant inhabitants appear to have evolved to a level of consciousness that allows them to perceive and question their circumstances.

Obviously, my next step must be that of making contact with them.

3.

THEY SAT IN HIS beat-up pickup truck at the side of the dirt road running through the desolate stretch of woods east of town.

"Would you stop it, Larry!" She pushed his hand away. "I told you, I saw a light! There's somebody out there!"

"Come on, Ella, in the middle of the woods? This time of night?"

Edging closer to her, he felt the ache that always came when she was nearby, brushing past him in the cafe, leaning too far over the counter when she served him.

"No, I said!" She pouted and leaned away against the door.

Irritation began to itch as he shifted his weight on the seat, creaking the springs. He turned on the one headlight that was still working and peered through his windshield at the narrow road making its way through trees and tangled undergrowth until it disappeared in the darkness waiting just beyond the reach of the headlight.

"There," he said. "Ain't nothing out there." He began edging back. "You're safe in here with me, Ella. Anybody messes with us," he reached behind and patted the rifle on the rack across his rear window, "and I just blow 'em away."

He nudged awkwardly against her in the dim light, his hand trying to make new inroads, until he saw her mouth drop open. She was staring intently ahead. Slowly, without speaking, she raised her hand and pointed her finger.

He looked through the windshield again and saw that a figure had emerged from the dark edge of the woods and was coming towards them with an odd, staggering motion back and forth on the road, like a sailor just off ship after a rough oceanic journey, trying to get his land legs again. He was carrying something that looked like a stick.

"What...the...hell...?" Larry reached behind and took the rifle off the rack. Working the bolt quickly, he put a round in the chamber and opened his door, stepping out onto the road and into the headlight so that whoever was approaching could see that he was armed and ready.

"Hold it right there!" he yelled, but the figure kept coming, until Larry was able to see more clearly what it was he was confronting. Walking somewhat more steadily now, the figure approaching him was a middle-aged man who was dressed in a dun-colored shirt and pants. It struck Larry that he had seen the man before, but he could not quite remember where or when. The man appeared to be contorting his face into different expressions, as though he were trying each of them out, stretching his mouth wide open, squinting his eyes tightly closed, looking aghast, delighted, saddened, puzzled.

"Who is it, Larry?" Ella had rolled the truck window down and was leaning out, her voice edged with concern.

"Don't know," said Larry. "Some crazy guy. Probably drunk." The figure was now just a few yards away. "Hold it, I said!" Larry pointed his rifle. "I ain't kidding, mister! You better stop right there."

The man finally stopped and began looking curiously at Larry. He leaned heavily on the piece of dead branch that he was using as a cane to keep his balance. "Which of us are you addressing?"

Larry glanced around uncomfortably, trying to see into the concealing darkness, and then focused on the man again.

"I'm talking to you, mister. What are you doing out here? What you got in mind?"

The question appeared to startle the man. "You don't know?" He leaned forward slowly and studied Larry intently, as though he were attempting to look inside him. "You *don't* know," he said, his surprise still showing. "Amazing."

Larry stepped out of the headlight, watching the man closely, and came back beside the truck to speak to Ella. When he looked up and saw that she was watching him, waiting to see what he would do, he thought it was time to take the matter decisively in hand. "Maybe I better just wing him a bit. Shoot him in the leg or something." He raised his rifle again toward the man.

"No, Larry! Don't be silly! He isn't doing anything!" She pushed open the truck door. "Let's get out of here. I don't like it here."

"Sure, Ella. Whatever you say." He turned back to the man. "All right, mister. On your way, before I change my mind."

The man straightened up and composed his face into a pleasant expression. Lifting his cane, he took two steps to the right and continued walking past Larry, who backed up a bit to keep his distance. Larry continued watching him, holding the rifle at ready, until the man disappeared into the darkness behind the truck.

"Come on, Larry," Ella said from inside the cab. "I got the creeps."

"Sure, Ella." Larry stepped up into the truck, smiling now as he thought of how Ella would have to admire him for protecting her from the crazy man on the road. He wondered for a moment if he really would have shot the guy, say if the guy had come at them in some scary way, or if the stick he was carrying had turned out to be a rifle.

"You're damn tootin'!" he told himself. Starting the truck,

he jammed it into gear and tromped on the gas pedal, spinning his wheels for Ella to hear that Larry was back in action again. Everybody on the desolate dirt road east of town had better get out of his way.

4.

When I asked Larry, Which of us are you addressing? it was evident that he had no accurate awareness of his own physical composition. An interesting phenomenon. His consciousness was floating on the surface of a multitude of life forms composing his physical structure, and yet he apparently assumed that only he was occupying his body. Within every one of the diversified cells that had accumulated to contain his presence, throughout every area of his interior tubular passageways, and on every external surface of his body, a host of mitochondrial and other symbiotic and parasitic forms of life were existing and interacting in large measure in ways that were needed to support his containment, and yet he appeared to be completely unaware of their presence.

Regardless of that notable deficiency, Larry's limited consciousness had nevertheless assumed control of his body's external actions. If I had given him the slightest encouragement, shown him the least provocation, he would have readily disorganized the containment of my consciousness, possibly even terminating my existence. A remarkable potential.

I will need to move among them with extreme caution.

5.

IT WAS A RATHER dusty and dreary small town, with visibly deteriorating houses staggered unevenly along the main street. At the center of the town, the commercial buildings had all been closed for hours, except for a solitary corner diner, where the light coming feebly through the front window into the deepening night intensified the sense of loneliness in anyone left standing on the street.

Inside, there was a man behind the counter and another on a stool talking with him. Two others at a table toward the rear were playing a game of cards. A blended aroma of variously cooked foods still lingered in the room from an earlier part of the evening.

When the door opened, the man behind the counter looked up. He was somewhat puffy-faced and overweight. His expression was not welcoming. Holding a rag that was questionably clean, he wiped the counter in front of one of the empty stools, as though indicating to the man who had just entered where he should sit. "Yeah?" he said, watching the man. "What can I get you?"

The others in the room had turned to check out the stranger. The men in the rear were dressed in work-shirts and dirty jeans. One of them wore a beat-up baseball cap with fishing flies and hooks stuck in it. Seeing nothing unusual, they went back to their game. The man sitting at the counter wore a sportcoat and slacks. He was young, with dark hair and complexion, and with sad, inquisitive eyes that he kept steadily on the man.

The man shaped his expression into a slight smile and sat on one of the stools. The counterman continued watching him, waiting for him to answer. When the man saw the picture on the wall behind the counter, he pointed at it. "How much would that cost?"

The counterman glanced at the picture. "Apple pie?"

The man nodded.

"Seventy-five cents. Is that what you want?"

"And that?" The man pointed at the cup in front of the young man sitting at the counter.

"Coffee is fifty cents," the counterman said. "Is that what you want? Pie and coffee?" He could feel his irritation rising. He was sure that he had seen this guy before. But he just couldn't place him.

"I must be hungry," the man said, touching his stomach. "But I do not have any money." He smiled apologetically. "A rather unfortunate oversight."

The counterman exchanged looks with the young man and then turned back to the stranger, his irritation peaking. "Then why the hell did you come in here? This ain't no soup kitchen."

"It's all right, Eddie," the young man at the counter said. "Give him some pie and coffee. I'll pay for it."

The counterman stared at the young man a moment with exaggerated disbelief, trying to decide if he should let it happen. Then he shook his head. "Mr. Soft-Touch himself," he said, and turned to reach for the apple pie in the glass case behind him.

As he was putting a slice of the pie onto a dish, the stranger reached out suddenly toward the young man and appeared to pluck something from the side of his head. The young man, feeling a shock, jerked his head back, surprised, and, with a frown, looked at the stranger. "Sorry," the stranger said, his bland features shaping themselves now into an apologetic look. "Was it static electricity? I thought you had a bit of fuzz caught there in your hair." The young man brushed his fingers through his hair and looked at his hand, but nothing was there.

The stranger then sat quietly until the pie and the coffee were put on the counter in front of him. Lifting a forkful to his mouth, he began chewing slowly, staring all the while down at the pie. He appeared to be concentrating on what he was doing, carefully considering each of his motions and the materials that had been placed before him. When he swallowed, he brightened and looked at the two men. "Good," he said.

"Best damn pie in the county," the counterman said, as though daring anyone to contradict him. He rubbed his rag on the counter again. "Not from around here, are you." It was not a question.

The man smiled again slightly. "You could say that."

"Then what brings you to these parts?" the counterman said, his voice still unpleasantly edged.

The young man on the nearby stool smiled slightly and swiveled slowly to face the stranger. "Would you believe that under his gruff exterior he's really a charming guy? But we do live in a small town, and anybody new here peaks our curiosity."

"I understand," the man said, and continued eating the pie.

They both watched him now, their curiosity not waning, until he had finished the pie and most of the coffee. He sat quietly then, as though thinking through the experience he had just undergone. "I am assuming," he said, as though to himself, "that, because my physical body required additional energy, I had no alternative but to ingest a number of elementary life forms."

The counterman stared at the stranger. "Cheeez..." he said,

turning to the young man. "He sounds like your kind of guy, Professor." He moved away, shaking his head, and went down the length of the counter to speak with the two men in the rear playing cards.

"Elementary life forms," the young man repeated, considering the remark as he continued watching the stranger. He smiled slightly, wondering if the man was kidding. "Well, let's see," he said, giving the man his full attention. "The pie was made of apples, the crust from grain, the coffee from beans. All of them, as you put it, were indeed elementary life forms."

"It was good of you to pay for them," the man said. He sat there a moment, studying the young man. "Perhaps I could do something for you in return."

Normally, the young man at this point would have turned back to the solitude of his own coffee, politely dismissing the offer, since it came from someone obviously down on his luck and on the road. But, for some reason, the stranger continued to hold his attention. "Such as?" he said, curious now about what the man might say.

"Perhaps," the man said, and he lifted his hand and moved it again, but slowly now, toward the young man's head, "by letting you know what actually happened that day. You have been wondering for so many years."

The young man frowned, "What do you mean?" and began to tip his head away from the approaching hand. The stranger paused a moment, lifting both hands with fingers spread to show that he was hiding nothing, and then reached slowly out once more until, with his index finger, he gently touched a spot above the young man's left temple.

At precisely the moment of touch, the young man jerked, as though suddenly aroused from a deep sleep, and then, with a startled look, he stared inwardly as an unwanted recollection began unfolding.

6.

THE WINDOW-SHADE WAS *still down in daylight, darkening the room. As she pulled the sheet up over her to keep in the smells that were still lingering, she listened to him singing now. "I've got you...under my skin. I've got you...deep in the hmmm of me." Until she heard the sound of the water in the bathroom. Now he would wash away her body and let it swirl down the drain.*

Pushing the sheet down from her, she felt the loss of her nakedness. Her clothes were draped across the dresser. She put them on slowly, finishing with her shoes, as he came out from the bathroom in his shorts, still singing. " I... saw... you... last... night... and... .got... that... ooooooold... feeling." He dressed quickly.

They left his apartment, and as they walked the few blocks to her street, she tried to get him to leave her, but he insisted on taking her nearer to her flat. When they turned the corner, she saw Les ahead, sitting on the curb, so he stopped and let her walk on alone.

"Time to go in now, Les," she said, smiling as she came up to him. "What have you got there?"

He was holding a jar in his lap with holes punched through the metal cap. "Spider." He looked toward the corner. "Who's that?"

She glanced around and saw him still standing there, watching. "Just a man, Les. Let's go in. Your father will be home soon."

Les got up from the curb. "Why is he looking?"

"I don't know, Les." She took his hand and started up the stairs. "Maybe he thinks he knows us."

"Does he?" Les said, looking up at her.

"No, Les." She didn't look down. "Not him."

Les played on the kitchen floor while she started supper, listening to her singing softly. "I want to be looooved, with inspiraaaation...."

And the plate-glass window at the front of the diner shattered into a thousand scattering pieces.

7.

"HOLY SHIT!" THE COUNTERMAN said. He hurried to the front of the diner, crunching glass shards underfoot. After looking around at the ragged edging of glass still in the window frame, he peered out through the opening into the night to see who or what had broken his window. In both directions, as far as he could make out, all of the windows facing the street appeared to be broken. Farther up the street, people were sticking their heads out through the window frames. They began to come out of their houses. "What was it, Mike?" he heard in the distance. "Sonic boom!" someone yelled. "Must have been a sonic boom!" Another voice answered. "I didn't hear any boom! What's going on here?"

The two card players had followed him, and they all stood there surveying the damage. One of the players, a small man with a large mustache, looked out the window and gestured to his friend. "Jesus, Jack, take a look! It's all up and down the street!"

The counterman turned back to the young man and the stranger still sitting at the counter. "Did you see what happened here, Les?" he said, his voice pitched high with stress. "Did you see what did it?"

The young man, Les, had not taken his eyes from the stranger, even when the window had shattered. He sat there, staring at the stranger with a look of bewilderment. "How in heaven's name did you...." He struggled visibly to control himself.

The stranger swiveled on his stool to face the men at the front of the diner. "Sorry. We were looking at something else."

"Les?" the counterman said, his suspicion of the stranger stronger now. It was too much of a coincidence.

Les glanced at the counterman and shook his head. The stranger had turned back again, smiling now with a touch of sympathy at the young man's confusion.

"It was some kind of a trick, wasn't it," Les said, trying hard to regain his sense of reason. "Some form of hypnosis, perhaps."

"And the window?" the stranger said.

"Somebody's going to pay for this!" the counterman said. He had begun to sweep the pieces of glass into a pile when he was jolted by a thought. "I'll have to sleep in here tonight, for Chrisake! Who's going to watch the place?" The card players tried to help by scraping the glass toward the pile with their shoes.

"You were sitting here right in front of me at the time," Les said. "You can't tell me that you had anything to do with that."

"Not directly," the stranger said. "That's true. But I must admit to having some responsibility."

"How so?" Les said, still half distracted by the confusion of his own thoughts.

The stranger studied him again for a moment and then appeared to reach a decision. "I'm pursuing someone, and he's sending me a sign that he knows I am here."

"A rock through the window?" Les said.

"There was no rock," the stranger said. "It was a vibrational force creating a molecular stress. We have brought a number of devices with us," he said, touching his belt. "They are designed mostly for our protection, but he is finding other uses for them. And I'm afraid that was just the beginning. He's determined to stop me."

"Who?" Les said, his confusion flaring up again. "Who

are you talking about?"

"Fedhisss." The man almost whispered the name, as though sharing a troublesome secret with Les. "I'm pursuing Fedhisss."

8.

STARING AT THE STRANGER sitting beside him at the counter, Les was still mentally struggling, for the childhood recollection that was slowly waning within him had extended outward beyond the range of any awareness he could have had at that early moment in his life. It had included not only the physical setting of her infidelity, which he had never seen, but also, apparently, her thoughts and emotions as she went through it. Impossible, he told himself. It must have been some self-hypnotic form of deception out of that emotionally disruptive part of his early life, brought out in some way by the suggestive remarks of the stranger and his unsettling gesture of touching Les's head. That must be it.

But his explanation, which he considered reasonable, was not, after all, a calming one. He had lived too long now with the sense that all associations with that childhood memory had long ago been stifled within him, pushed out of memory's range.

Apparently, though, some locked gate had been opened a bit, for another memory slowly came to him, not as intense or as immediate as the first. He was four years old and under the covers in the large bed in his parent's bedroom, still awake and waiting for his mother. They lived in a small flat on the second floor behind a corner tavern in a run-down neighborhood. It was winter, and his father had come down with a bad cold. Not wanting to keep his mother awake, his father had decided to sleep in Les's room. Les would sleep with his mother in his parent's room. She had told Les, with a smile, how much she hated to climb into a cold bed, and she said how nice it was going to be to find that he had made it all warm and toasty for her.

Lying there in the bed, he was troubled by the thought of how much bigger she was, and so he slid way down under the covers, down until his feet reached to the bottom of the bed. Feeling the cold sheets on his legs, he tried to warm with his own thin body all the places that would touch hers.

His mother finally came in. "You still awake?" She left the light off as she undressed quickly and came to the bed. "It's getting late. We'd better get to sleep."

"I tried to warm it," Les said, watching as she got under the covers.

"Oh, yes," she said softly. "How wonderful. All warm and toasty." She slid in beside him and took him in her arms, holding him close. "What a love you are."

Comfortably pressed against the side of her body, feeling safe now for the night, he remembered clearly his final dreamy thought as he melted slowly into sleep. He wanted... always...to be this close to her.

It was true, he realized, the memory, and why her leaving had hurt so much. She had always been there for him, his source of warmth among the many bitter winds that blew through the dingy streets of his inner-city world. And then, one day, she was gone, without any warning or explanation, just disappearing from his life, never to be seen again. It was more than he, at that early age, had been able to handle. And so something within him had closed a curtain across that part of his life, leaving him alone on this side of the darkness.

As the daily life that moved around him grew cold and pale, he turned to the one refuge that remained open to him. Every Saturday morning, for as long as he could remember, his father, who was an avid reader, had taken him to a local branch of the city's public library system. Les discovered early that there were different worlds existing between the covers of books, mythical lands with fascinating individuals, worlds where good and evil were clearly defined, and good always triumphed by the end of the story. Les learned to lose himself within the appealing warmth and brightness of these imaginative realms. But as he moved on into high school, his reading began to take on a new task, for within the mythical books were not only adventures, but reasoned explorations of the human motivations that impelled the characters into their acts of good and evil. Les was now drawn into other books, the classic works of fiction from his own and other countries that appeared to present the world and the people within it as they really were. *Anna Karenina. Sons and Lovers. Heart of Darkness. The Way of All Flesh. Madame Bovary*. Les explored a multitude of fictional worlds, wanting to know what drove the characters within them into their so often regretful acts.

With a scholarship and a part-time job, he made his way through college, and then on through graduate school, moving across an ever-widening range of subjects in the humanities and the sciences, discovering a multitude of books that claimed to describe the world objectively. But after so many years of searching, so many books where the front cover was opened with high expectations and the back cover closed with deep disappointment, he could apparently arrive at only one conclusion: that there was, after all, no meaning to life, no direction, no purpose, that not only his immediate world but the entire known universe could be characterized, as one author put it, by its "pitiless indifference." If that was the nature of life, he finally decided, then so be it. Les settled into that belief, with only one permanent scar still within him. Beneath the flow of his daily existence, just beyond the range of his waking awareness, a single thought, wrapped in determination, continued to shape the nature and direction of his life. Wherever he might find himself, whatever he might end up doing, he would never let another woman hurt him that badly again.

He thought of Anne then, sitting behind the desk in the library at the university, the warm, shy smile that lit her face whenever she saw him, the incredibly sensuous softness of her mouth when they had first kissed. Until recently, they had regularly been spending their evenings together. But then he had sensed the increasing appeal that she was making to him, opening her nature to him, wanting him to come in. He, in response, had felt the resistance building within him, gently urging her back a bit. It had worked well with the women before Anne, the inviolable space he had insisted upon maintaining around himself. But as the time that they were spending together had grown, Anne had simply continued to draw closer. With a touch of fear, as he felt the distance between them closing too quickly, he had suddenly turned away and without any explanation began to avoid her, confusing and saddening her.

With the touch of despair that always accompanied it, he recalled the passage in *The Brothers Karamozov*. After pondering the question "What is hell?" Father Zossima reveals "that it is the suffering of being unable to love."

And here was this man sitting calmly on the stool, watching Les with apparent interest. The man had somehow caused Les to bring up all the hurt again. For what reason? To what end? What could this rather bland looking individual possibly know about human nature beyond the knowledge that Les had already gathered from some of the greatest minds on earth?

9.

HAVING LOOKED MORE CLOSELY now at two particular representatives, Larry and Les, I have confirmed that human beings, in their waking moments, consider themselves to be existing as completely separate individuals. Isolated in a small raft of self-awareness that is floating on the surface of an oceanic consciousness (I do enjoy their word play), they paddle as best they can among the winds and waves, but rarely, if ever, do they attempt to venture beneath the surface. Each of them does indeed possess a separate, individualized grouping of living brain cells. But they apparently remain unaware that they are extensions of a larger consciousness existing as a single entity seeking to extend its awareness of the world within which it has been awakened. Eventually every individual brain is permanently disorganized, losing its capacity to contain consciousness. But the still accumulating totality of active brain cells around the planet is maintaining a deeper, a vaster consciousness.

With all that human beings could comprehend about their natures and the universe around them by delving into that greater depth, they appear to be intent upon experiencing their world only within the feeble glow of their own waking awareness.

What a strange species.

And Fedhisss is loose among them.

10.

Along the main street, the street-lamps lit a row of wide-ly spaced places, like stepping-stones through the benighted town. Just beyond the commercial buildings, people were still lingering in front of their houses. A few were looking up intently into the night sky.

Directly across the street, in the darkness between two buildings, a figure stood motionless, watching the diner.

In an apartment on the second floor of one of the buildings, a lamp near the window was clicked on, and a rectangle of light shone down on the figure, revealing a middle-aged man of average height and build and appearance. The man, dressed in a dun-colored shirt and pants, glanced up at the light and then stepped backwards slightly into darkness again.

Anticipating the pleasure he would derive from doing so, he brought to mind the event that had just occurred and fractured it into individual words. "Oh, yes, that was good. The shattering was good. There is nothing as beautiful as a shattering. The tiny bits of flying glass catching and reflecting the light as they twirled and tumbled through the air in a sparkling multitude of erratic paths. And the ending, yes, that was good, too, as they landed and spread out in such a delightful disarray. It was a most beautiful warning. There will be no room for doubt now.

"If he does not give up his pursuit, I will *shatter* him, and any life forms around him to some considerable distance."

11.

WHAT WAS GOING ON here? Les's instincts were telling him to get out of there, to put some distance between himself and the stranger, and the odd things that were happening, to get away from all of it—whatever it was. And there, he recognized, was the problem. He couldn't quite grasp what was going on. And within his confusion he could sense a tinge of fear, an elemental fear of the unknown, embodied somehow by the man sitting too calmly beside him.

Leaving his stool at the counter, Les motioned his good-bye to the still distraught counterman and started to leave the diner, assuming that the stranger would stay behind. But the man stood up and came after him, apparently going to follow him out. Near the door to the diner, the card player wearing the fish-hooked baseball cap was bent over, using a piece of cardboard to pick up pieces of glass. As he passed by, the stranger casually reached out and touched the side of the card player's head. The card player jerked back, as though jolted by an electric shock, and then stood up and stared at the stranger.

"Sorry," the stranger said. "Must have been static electricity." He continued out of the diner behind Les.

Outside on the sidewalk, Les paused a moment, turning to the man who had followed him. "I have a class to teach in the morning," he said, smiling slightly. "It's time I went home. Good luck to you." He set off at a brisk pace toward his apartment, attempting simply to walk away. But the man kept up with him, matching him step for step, while frowning slightly, apparently at the workings of his own thoughts.

Glancing hurriedly at the man, disconcerted again by the man's behavior, Les came to a full stop and faced him. "Look," he said, "I have no idea who you are, and I don't know what you are up to, but whatever it is, I don't wish to be involved. Now you can either go your own way and leave me alone, or I'll be forced to call the local police and have them check you out. It's up to you."

They stood on the sidewalk, staring at each other, Les guardedly watching the man, while the man continued to look at Les with a focused interest that did not appear to waver, even under the threat of the police being called. As Les studied the man's face, that bland expression, those common features, he recognized that it would be difficult if he had to describe him. There was nothing that really distinguished his appearance. He could be anyone. The idea, for some vague reason, made Les all the more uncomfortable.

"I understand your confusion," the stranger said, his voice remaining calm. "But whether you wish it or not, you have already become involved. This town and its people." The man gestured around him at the street stretching off in both directions, taking in the few people still out on their sidewalks who had come together into small groups and were talking softly and pointing toward their broken front windows. "You are attached to them in many ways. Much more than you realize." The stranger's face darkened. "Fedhisss will quickly gain the capacity to harm them."

Les could feel his impatience rising. "What are you saying? That you are with the police? That you are chasing some madman?" He tried to keep his voice under control. "If you were with the police, you'd have some identification on you.

27

And you certainly wouldn't be roaming around in the night without any money in your pocket, telling stories about somebody with an obviously phoney name who is going to harm the people of this town."

The man nodded slowly, as though agreeing with Les. "I understand," he said. "But Fedhisss is a very real threat, I assure you. He has already inflicted substantial damage across a large area just before he came here."

"Sure," Les said, smirking. Why, he wondered, was he giving this odd man any attention at all? The man was obviously on the road, down on his luck, some kind of a tramp. Was he trying for a handout? "And why haven't I heard of this extensive damage? We have pretty good coverage of the world's news every evening."

The man paused a moment, as though reaching another decision. "It was not on this planet."

Les watched the man for a moment as he took this in. Then he heard himself laughing nervously as he grappled mentally with the sense of how to respond to this astonishing claim. Clearly, the man must be unbalanced.

Rather than increasing Les's discomfort, however, it gave him the feeling, with some sense of relief, that he should not be unkind. "Ah," he said, nodding his own agreement. "On another planet, of course. I should have realized that. But I simply can't help with that. It's really beyond me. You'll have to handle it on your own. And so I must tell you good night again, and wish you the best of luck."

The man had raised his hand, and, with his index finger extended, was reaching out again for the side of Les's head.

"Oh, no!" Les said, backing away quickly. "I've already seen that trick."

"I need to share something with you," the man said. He held his hand out again to show Les that it was empty. "It's only a touch. Are you afraid of the truth?"

As the man's hand approached, Les found himself unable to move, caught between his wanting to avoid the touch, to avoid having something unpleasant take place again within him, and his intense curiosity of how the man was able to do it. It was, after all, only a touch.

As the man's finger made contact with the side of Les's head, he was startled again as a scene flashed into view within him, a setting unlike any he had ever known, a city, although not really a city, a large area of, not houses, but of structures that had apparently been erected for something to live with-in. But whoever or whatever had occupied the structures was nowhere in sight, leaving an eerie silence, like the after-scene of the towns and cities around Chernobyl. And yet it was unlike anything on this earth. The light falling across the scene was casting shadows in two directions, as though there were two suns, and the empty space above the area seemed to be hovering on the edge of visibility, moving erratically in and out of an almost material existence, heightening the sense of some profound disruption having taken place, of space itself having somehow been elementally shattered.

Les jerked his head away, trying to free himself from the view. "Who are you?" he said, plaintively appealing for something that would allow him to understand what was happening.

"At the present time," the man answered, looking down at himself, "I am someone like you." He smiled slightly at the comparison. "With a few additions that always remain as a basic part of my organized energy."

"That place I just saw," Les persisted. "It was some kind of hypnotic illusion, wasn't it? You don't expect me to believe that it wasn't?"

"Yes," the man said calmly. "I do. It was on the last planet where Fedhisss and I landed, the second step we had taken to fulfill the purpose of our journey, to seek out and categorize new forms of life within the universe." His face remained expressionless, but he continued watching Les closely. "It is extremely important that you listen now to what I am about to tell you. Fedhisss and I have been traveling together in twin vessels for mutual security. Our first landing established that our vessels worked as they were designed to do, and that we were evidently going to survive our experimental journey. It gave us both a great sense of accomplishment in having so dramatically extended our capacities for exploration. But that was all changed during our second landing, cast into a shadow by a sudden alteration that occurred in Fedhisss. Some ensuing sense of power descended upon him, a sense that our own existence had now become superior to all others. Fedhisss no longer wanted simply to explore and categorize new life forms. Now he wanted to judge them. Were they worthy of survival? Did they deserve to exist? Much to my dismay, he concluded that the life forms on the last planet were developing in a direction that he considered to be superfluous, with no evident direction or purpose, a useless bit of clutter in that part of the universe that needed cleaning out." The man shook his head slightly, obviously pained by the recollection. "As you have seen, he was terribly destructive to the inhabitants."

Les was caught a moment by the story and the expression on the man's face. But then, with an effort, he mentally shook himself loose. "This is ridiculous!" he said, his voice rising. "Do you seriously expect me to believe that you're from another planet, some extraterrestrial creature who has chosen to drop in and chat with me a bit, as you stand here in front of me, so obviously just another human being?"

"Just another human being," the man repeated, as though considering the sound of the words. But then his expression darkened. "You saw what happened to the diner window and the windows up and down this street. That was only a warning. Not only to me, but to everyone throughout this area. If it helps you at all, then think of me as being with the police and chasing a madman. That would not be far from the truth. Whatever the case, I need your help."

"What do you mean?" Les said. "What kind of help? And who is this person with the peculiar name that you say you are chasing?" Why, Les thought, am I having this insane conversation? Why don't I simply walk away? "And what is your—how should I put it so that it doesn't sound stupid to me—your real name?"

"I am called Urr," the man said. "And the man I am pursuing is called Fedhisss."

"Keep talking," Les said, wanting to catch the man in some obvious lie or some inadvertent remark that would reveal the foolishness of it all.

"What would you like me to say?"

Les thought a moment. "You said that you each had an experimental vehicle that you used to arrive here on Earth?"

A police car came slowly up the street, with two officers in the front seat looking out at the broken windows. Les and the stranger stood quietly, watching the car as it passed and made its way further along the street until it finally turned off out of sight. "Yes," the stranger said, "that is how we came here."

All right, Les thought, and then carefully added, "But you are on foot now, walking around. Does that mean that your vehicle is nearby?"

"In the woods to the east beyond the edge of town."

"Can I also assume then," Les said, keeping his voice calm, "that, since you are so intent on convincing me that you are telling me the truth, you would have no objection to showing me the vehicle?"

He smiled politely at the man. Gotcha!

12.

HUMAN BEINGS ARE WILLING to entertain the notion that other forms of life may be present within the universe. But they usually picture them as being unpleasantly if not repulsively different, and desirous (note the irony) of feeding with uncontrolled ferocity on the dominant inhabitants to be found here. When they imagine a superior form of consciousness intellectually and technologically advanced within some distant civilization, they generally envision it to be in a future phase of their own development. To think otherwise would require them to question the efficiency of their own peculiar evolutionary development. But they appear to be comfortably unconcerned about the direction in which their flesh is flowing.

13.

THEY HAD MADE THEIR way to Les's apartment to get his car so that they could drive out east of town. Les had to admire how cool the man was staying as his bluff was being called. He was curious to see at what point the man's facade would crack, as what moment the man's story would collapse under the weight of its own foolishness. But he also recognized, beneath his curiosity, a compelling need to disprove the man, to wipe away the upsetting thoughts and images the man had raised in Les with a simple touch. It was only a touch. What was going on here?

After leaving the town and then driving more slowly along the narrow road that cut through the woods, the man had finally told Les to stop the car. Les pulled off to the side of the road and parked. He had brought along a flashlight, which he gave to the man as they started off into the woods. He wanted the man to lead the way so that Les could trail behind him, determined to stay on his guard. He was unsure of how the man would react when his lie was exposed.

The flashlight jiggling along the path reflected off the leaves and branches of the undergrowth, silhouetting the man as he strode ahead. As the woods closed in around them, Les became increasingly troubled. How far away from the road did this man expect him to go?

The darkness pervading the woods around them, eerily silent, appeared to intensify as they moved further into it.

Les was about to call a halt and turn back when the man abruptly stopped. Turning to Les, he gestured with the beam of the flashlight.

Les cautiously peered around the man and—Good Lord! What was it? A strange ovoid-shaped object, its surface glistening metallically as the light moved upon it. It had a transparent dome at the top. Les took the flashlight from the man and directed it into the dome, which shielded an interior compartment that was apparently designed for a single occupant. The branches and undergrowth around the object remained unbroken. Considering its size, there was no way that it could have arrived there in the middle of the woods, except from above. It was unlike anything Les had ever seen. The Air Force? NASA? As he studied the strange vehicle, it gave him a sinking feeling, a mixture of certitude and confusion, that it was not of this world.

He turned questioningly to the man.

The man smiled politely at Les. "Gotcha!" he said.

Sitting at the kitchen table in his small apartment, Les was still deeply shaken as he stared at Urr.

"And you say that you can be stored like electricity in a battery as you make your way across space?"

"Not a good comparison," Urr said. "Electricity within a battery would be too disorganized a form of energy. Life is essentially an ordering. You are essentially an ordering of your elements. But not, I should add, as you might first think, for you are more than the sum of your parts."

"What do you mean?" Les said, frowning.

Urr was silent for a moment as he considered how to answer. "If I were to gather together all of the constituent elements composing your physical body, and then arranged them exactly as they are now arranged, the consciousness that would then become evident within that containment would not arise simply out of those organized physical elements. Think, instead, at least partly, of a radio, although that, too, as a comparison has its problems. Different life forms, in the way they are physically organized, are attuned at their deepest levels to different frequencies of consciousness."

Les shook his head in perplexity. "Since you are obviously a human being now, what are you able to see that I'm not capable of seeing? What range of experience, what different frequency of consciousness, as you put it, what—"

"Look," the man said, "there by the leg of the table."

Les glanced down and saw a small blue beetle running along the kitchen floor.

"That tiny creature," the man said, "is exuding a little aura of awareness as it makes its way across the expanse of the linoleum. Notice how it is moving in a straight line, unswerving, as though it were intent upon pursuing an important journey. It is completely unaware of you watching it. It does not have the capacity to perceive you. If you got up now from your chair, walked over and stepped on it as it hurried unsuspectingly along, it would never know what force had obliterated it. Perhaps, for a split second, it would perceive the darkening bottom of your foot descending above it, but even then it would remain ignorant of the nature of the thoughtful force about to destroy it."

The beetle continued running away from the table along its evidently chosen path.

"As you watch that creature moving across your floor, you should be able to recognize that you are existing in a comparable state, scurrying along some line of your own, assuming that you are heading somewhere, with perhaps a somewhat more advanced aura of awareness."

"*Perhaps* more advanced than a beetle?" Les said, smiling slightly.

Urr was studying Les now, waiting to see how he would respond.

Les returned his gaze as he considered Urr's comparison. "What you are saying, if I understand you correctly, is that I, as a typical human being, am essentially and self-deceptively ignorant."

Urr nodded slowly, as though he wished it were otherwise. "Considerably more than you realize," he said. Then his face brightened. "But not as much as you were only a moment ago," he added. "I find that somewhat encouraging."

Les was stung a bit by the criticism. "Tell me," he said, watching in turn for Urr's response. "Might there also be someone watching you as I have been watching the beetle?"

Urr laughed with obvious pleasure. "Very good!" he said. "There is absolutely no reason to think otherwise."

"And you are telling me," Les said, "that, as I could so easily have stepped on the beetle, Fedhisss can step on me?"

"Unfortunately, it may not only be on you. Fedhisss will be judging your species. In his eyes, do you deserve to exist as a life form? Here, on your peculiar planet, your life form is new to us, a life form actually capable of destroying its own members, in a world of other life forms destroying each other." Urr paused again and then shook his head slowly, as though puzzled by his own thoughts. "This is a remarkable place."

He saw the troubled look on Les's face. "Or should I say," he added, smiling now, "it's an interesting place to visit, but I wouldn't want to live here."

"What exactly is it that you want from me?" Les said. "You already have access to everything within my mind, including, apparently, even to the thoughts and feelings of other individuals I have known." Les explored with his finger the side of his own head. "How can you do that? It's still too unreal." He struggled a moment to bring his confusion back under some semblance of control. "What else could I possibly add to what you already know?"

"What I already know," Urr said, "is considerably less than you might imagine. My only consolation is that Fedhisss is in the same state. He and I are in a race now to understand the nature of the life forms on this planet, and particularly why they are capable of destroying each other, for he will likely make use of that information both to stop me, and in judging you." He frowned slightly. "His judgment will include a central question, one that I am sure perplexes us both." Pausing a moment, he considered Les carefully, as though beginning his own evaluation. "Can you tell me how it is possible for you to be such a murderous creature?"

"Me?" Les said, feeling somewhat indignant. "What do you mean? I've never killed anyone."

"Ah," Urr said. "I see." His face brightened again. "You have just given me the answer to my question."

"I don't understand," Les said.

"Let me illustrate, then, with something I gathered earlier, from one of the two representatives of your life form who were at the rear of the diner."

"The two men playing cards?"

"Yes." He reached forward to touch Les's head. "Tell me," he said, as Les looked anxiously at the approaching hand. "Assume for a moment that you had come here to explore the nature and quality of human life so that you could decide if such creatures were worthy of their existence. Consider these two representatives now, and tell me. How would *you* judge them? Would you allow them to continue living?"

Les winced as Urr made contact.

14.

LEW BROUGHT THE ROD back, flicked his wrist, and watched the line curve out into the morning sunlight. It plopped into the still water. He was a thin man, with a mustache too bushy for his narrow face. At the other end of the rowboat, Jack shifted his weight to cast in the opposite direction. The rowboat rocked, and ripples moved out until the shoreline, reflected in the glassy lake, began to waver.

"I tell you, Lew, it was enough to make me question the makeup of this whole cock-eyed world. I mean, have you ever had a cat?"

Lew shook his head, staying silent, and began to reel in slowly, a V of water following his line toward the boat. He had a deep respect for the rituals of fishing.

"Then I can't really tell you the shock of it all. Not really, I mean. You've got to see it for yourself. This small soft creature that purrs when you pet her and rubs up against your leg."

Lew glanced with a frown as Jack began to reel in with his ratchet on.

"Like just yesterday," Jack said, "she came walking up to me, lazy as can be, with a field mouse hanging out of her mouth. You know what I mean? Those tiny little ones with big ears? Like Mickey Mouse." He put his rod on his lap and held his hands up to his head, fingers spread wide. He waited until Lew looked.

"I know it's the Law of Nature and all that, but this one was alive. I mean, it wasn't even dead. And up she comes and drops it right in front of me. Like a gift, maybe. Like maybe she thought

I needed a mouse. And naturally, when that little fellow hits the ground, off he goes, his little legs working as fast as they can, and—Hold it!" He jerked his rod hard. The line snapped through the water and then went slack. "Ha!" He reeled in quickly. "Almost had him." He baited his hook again and cast out into the same area. Lew brought his line in, held up the rod to check the bait, and then cast again on his own side.

"Like I was saying, when that mouse got about three feet away, quick as you could see she pounced on it once more, brought it back, and dropped it again in front of me. Then she just sat there. Looking bored, mind you. And you know what that little mouse did?"

Lew pursed his lips, his mustache bristling, as he tried to reel in noiselessly.

"Do you know what that little mouse did? He stood straight up, right under her face, and looked up at her sitting there, looming over him, and he started to chatter at her, squeaking and squealing up at her, like he was telling her just what he thought of her. 'Why don't you pick on someone your own size, you big, black, fat-faced bully, you!'" Jack chuckled at the thought of it. "And do you know what she did, Lew?"

Lew shook his head resignedly.

"Standing right there was that little mouse, chattering out his heart to her, asking up at her why she was doing such a terrible thing to him, and she just lifts up one of her paws, as casual as you please, and gives it a lick with her tongue. Ho hum! Like she doesn't even know this little fellow's even talking."

"Strike!" Lew cried. His rod bowed as he began to reel in.

Jack watched him play with it for a few moments, but his mind was elsewhere. "And it's not just field mice, either, Lew. It's moles, and chipmunks, and squirrels, and rabbits—even a full-grown one! You know how small she is. She had to drag it home. Couldn't even carry it. Wow!" he said, remembering the torn, dead rabbit.

Lew moved the tip of his rod back and forth, trying to keep a sense of the drag he needed, as he played the fish toward the rowboat.

"And when it's nighttime, Lew, you'd never believe it." Jack had stopped reeling, and his line was slowly settling toward the bottom. "I mean, if we leave the porch light on, we'll hear her jumping up on the screen door, catching June bugs and moths and things. The crackling those June bugs make! When she eats them, I mean. You'd never believe it."

Lew took the rod in one hand, held high, as he worked the fish over the net, and then lifted. Curved in the bottom of the net was a small rainbow.

"Looks big enough to keep," Jack said.

Lew nodded, wet his hand, and took the fish off the hook. He dropped it into a metal pail half full of lake water and watched it a moment. It floated in place, moving its fins.

"Have you ever seen a baby robin, Lew?" Lew shook his head. Jack watched him baiting his hook again. "Maybe I should try one of your grasshoppers." He tilted a tin-can on the seat beside him. "These worms aren't wiggling much anymore."

Lew worked the point of the hook carefully down from the thorax to the abdomen. The grasshopper flailed its legs and then took hold of the hook and spit tobacco-juice on Lew's finger. He wiped it on his pants, settling himself again, and then cast out in the same direction.

Jack continued watching. His line now went straight down into the water toward the bottom. "That baby robin, Lew. I mean, it wasn't only one. There were three of them in the nest in that big maple out in front of the house. I didn't think she'd find them at first. But then last week I walked out into the garage, and there she was. With this big baby bird. Lew, you'd have to see it. I mean, it was still kind of fluffy with baby feathers, and as plump and pretty as you could think. And there it was, hanging out of her mouth, its head flopped down all stretched and dead looking. Hey!"

He felt a tug on his line and jerked up. The rod stayed bowed this time, so he started to reel in, at a steady speed.

"When she dropped that one right in front of me and headed back out to the front yard, I chased her, but she made it up the tree. I had to stand there, looking up, and watch her stroll out onto that limb again, as slow and as unconcerned as you please, while the mother and father bird were flapping all over the tree and down onto the grass and screaming and screetching away at her, 'Murder! Murder!' And do you know, in the middle of all that commotion she even stopped half-way out on that limb to look around a little, like maybe she was enjoying the view. Hey!"

He had reeled in too far, lifting the fish up out of the water, so he swung his pole over the boat. The fish fell off the hook into the bottom of the boat and started flopping, until he managed to hold it down with his shoe. He picked it up quickly and dropped it into the pail. It was at least two inches longer than the first catch.

Lew was concentrating intently upon reeling in his line.

Jack paused a moment over the pail. "I tell you, Lew, it's enough to make you question who's running this whole mixed-up shebang."

At noon-time they rowed in to shore for lunch. After Jack had built a small fire, he watched Lew prepare the fish. Holding each trout near the tail, alive again in his hand, Lew whacked it against the side of a tree. It quivered and stiffened. Their color was still brilliant in the noon sunlight, and Jack smacked his lips. "Nothing like it, right out of the water."

Lew slit them carefully, from the vent to the jaw. He scraped out the insides, the gills and the tongue, and then threw the mess back into the lake.

"They're beauties," Jack said. "But not much more than a mouthful." He reached into his knapsack and brought out two sandwiches wrapped in waxpaper. "Good thing we brought these. You want to trade one?"

Lew wiped his hands and took out his sandwiches. "What you got?"

"Ham and cheese. What about you?"

"Corned-beef," Lew said.

After they had traded, Jack took a big bite out of Lew's sandwich. Looking out over the lake, rippling now from a light breeze, he sniffed in a breath mixed with the smell of gutted fish and held it a moment. Then he sighed with deep satisfaction around his mouthful of slaughtered steer.

15.

LES STRUGGLED BACK TO his own thoughts out of a confusing swirl of worms and grasshoppers and fish and flesh, lingering images of death, and two men casually, complacently inflicting it or devouring its remains. "What would you have me say?" he complained. "Of course they deserve to exist. I know them both. They're decent men."

Urr nodded, as though in agreement. "And you, too, Les. You are unquestionably convinced that you are basically a decent man. You have gained little, if any, awareness, throughout the course of your life, of just how pervasively destructive you actually are to other life forms."

"So what's your point? I should become a vegetarian?"

Urr shrugged slightly. "You would still be consuming other life forms."

"Oh, sure," Les said, throwing up his hands. "Then why don't I just stop eating?"

Urr apparently gave the remark serious consideration.

"Forget it," Les said. "I'm not about to starve myself to death. Eating is a necessary part of our existence. It's a *natural* part," Les stressed.

"Yes," Urr said. "And that is exactly the problem, for Fed-hisss will also consider it so. He will see you still mired in the mechanical workings of the universe, functioning at a level of consciousness beneath any that he would value."

Sitting there in his kitchen, trying to take it all in, Les

could almost hear the silence that now pervaded the room. How, he wondered, could he possibly grasp, with any sense of reality, the things that Urr was telling him?

Urr nodded his own understanding. "You do not want to recognize a truth that you find too upsetting."

"It's not every day," Les said, "that I'm faced with the idea that some distorted being with a destructive nature has arrived here from another world to decide if we should continue existing. It's simply too unbelievable."

"Perhaps, at the moment," Urr said. "But Fedhisss will soon make his presence more evident."

"How soon?" Les said. He thought of the many people he knew throughout the town. They would be going about their lives now, watching television, putting their kids to bed, having their evening snack, their nightcap, lights out. And then he thought of Anne, home from the library, alone now in her apartment as she settled in for the night. Alone? The knot in his stomach tightened.

"There is a safety feature on our vehicles," Urr said. "Periodically, they signal their location. When they do, I will know exactly where Fedhisss has landed. If I am able to reach his vehicle before he does, I will be able to send it back without him."

"Leaving him here?" Les said, his voice rising. "Stranding him here to roam about and do as he pleases?"

"Fedhisss will never willingly give up his vehicle," Urr said. "He will act to stop me before that time."

"But what can you do to stop him?"

"If I can make contact with him, a single touch, I am equipped to stop him."

"What does that mean?"

"He would no longer be able to control his vehicle. And whatever devices he may have with him will be deactivated. He will have no choice but to return with me."

"Or stay here?" Les said, upset again at the possibility.

"No." Urr shook his head. "He knows by now that, if he did, the present containment of his consciousness would eventually decompose, and his energy would naturally and unwillfully dissipate, terminating his existence. Fedhisss will not let that happen. He would never accept such a terrible fate."

"You mean," Les said, with a wry smile, "the common fate experienced by all life forms on this planet."

"Yes," said Urr, frowning now. "And I am deeply puzzled by your ability to smile at the thought of it."

Les shrugged. "What other choice do we have?" Urr seemed about to answer, but Les continued. "You said that Fedhisss will act before his vehicle signals its location. When will that be?"

"Here?" Urr said, considering the time. "By six o'clock tomorrow evening."

"Tomorrow!" Les could feel his tension mounting. "How can you possibly stop him in such a short time? You don't even know where he is right now."

"I know that he is in this immediate area," Urr said. "And I know he will be seeking for information about this planet and its life forms, and for certain materials he will need to stop me from pursuing him. Fedhisss likes to....How should I say it? He likes to tinker with things. Particularly with anything that manipulates orderly forms of energy. He has a talent for building devices that can do unusual things. He's very creative, really, in his own way. So I would begin to focus my search for him with two questions to you."

"Yes?" Les said.

"First," Urr said, "what is the population of this town?"

Les tried to recall. "I believe it's somewhere between seven and eight thousand."

"Then think for a moment," Urr said. "If you were Fedhisss, with all the terrible capabilities of a human being now at your disposal, where would you go, in this particular area, to discover a practical way to destroy"—he opened his hands, as though hefting the corporeal weight of the town—"say, ten thousand people?"

16.

IT IS AN INTERESTING characteristic they display, their thoughtless acceptance of a seemingless harmless metaphor—"the food chain"—which they frequently use as a scientifically descriptive label. How easily they have been taught to accept, calmly and unquestioningly, such an astonishing cruelty of mortal existence. Every minute of every day throughout this entire planet, life forms are ripping apart and devouring other life forms to survive. Human beings label, categorize, and rank them into a thoughtfully conceived order that they designate "the food chain," and then discuss the concept off-handedly—Who is higher on it? Who is lower?—as though they are simply describing another natural phenomenon. When will the next lunar eclipse occur? What will the weather be like tomorrow?

How can they be so complacent about that ravenous feast? Because they are presently sitting at the head of the table. But life on this planet, across its history, has apparently been playing a game of musical chairs. How will they fare when they must rise at the sound of the next tune?

Generally, they manage, at least during their waking days, to consider themselves, individually, to be an exception to any form of mortal dissolution, until they are forced by circumstances to recognize their vulnerability. But even then, their first reaction is one of astonished disbelief.

I include here a conversation I had with Les on the way

back to his apartment from the woods, when I told him that Fedhisss would seriously consider sterilizing his planet.

"You mean, kill all of the germs on it?"

"No, not just the germs. I am talking about all life forms on this planet."

"Everything?"

"Yes."

"Including human beings?"

"Particularly so."

"You're not serious?"

"I am dead serious, if I may put it that way. I do like your jargon."

He stared at me. "And you expect me to believe it?" I had to smile as I shook my head.

17.

During the remainder of the night in Les's apartment, Les had settled Urr on the couch and had then tried with little success to get some sleep before the morning came. But he had tossed and turned through most of the night, struggling with the question that Urr had posed. How could he seriously be expected to find some way to kill so many people? To kill even one person? It was simply not in him to do so. But there were moments, as he hovered on the edge of sleep, when he found himself wandering among darker urges in some deeper realm within his mind and wondering how strongly they would rise up if it came down to a question of his own survival....

The end of all life on Earth? It was a concept that was simply too far beyond his mental capacities to grasp. If someone had told him that there had been a major earthquake, and that California, its lands and buildings and its entire population, had been split off from the continent and had fallen into the Pacific Ocean, completely disappearing from sight, he would find himself just as incapable of mentally grasping the reality of that occurrence. He could think of it happening. He could even struggle to imagine it happening. But he knew that eventually it would strike him as simply unbelievable, beyond the bounds of his comprehension. How, then, could he deal with the end of all life on Earth? Simply unbelievable.

And what could he possibly do about it, even if the threat were true? Aliens, come to Earth. He almost laughed as he thought of all the reported UFO sightings, and the alien abduction stories that had made the rounds. People so desperately wanting such things to be true, desiring so strongly for something, anything, to break the routines of their daily, hum-drum lives. And here it was, apparently, happening to him. He was being asked to take part in a conflict going on between two...what? With one of them considering whether or not to end all life on Earth.

Could a single being do that? Les remembered the devastation he had seen on the other planet, and the eerie feeling he had experienced that some form of life once existing there had been completely destroyed. But could that possibly happen here? Or were there larger universal forces at work that would determine the outcome, forces that would simply not allow the obliteration of all life forms on Earth? Les did not believe in any formal concept of a God, but he could not deny the unsatisfied yearning within himself for something beyond his own existence, some being, or, more likely, some unfolding pattern within the workings of the universe that, however chaotically it might presently appear, was moving everything toward some distant point of meaningful fulfillment.

Or was it all simply happening? No pattern, no meaning, as he had concluded years ago, only a mechanically evolving universe continuing to grind its gears. There was nothing yet that he had experienced to suggest otherwise.

Sometime during the fitful night, it came to him, where the answer to Urr's question might be found, and where Fedhisss would go to find what he was seeking. Of course, Les thought...too obvious...and he was able finally to drift off...into a discomforting dream.

He was standing on a lawn in a large park across the street from the city library. Looking up, he could clearly see the craggy asteroid that was speeding through space on a collision course with the city. Running across the street, he hurried into the library to find the book that contained the information he needed to prevent the collision. The library was huge, and the walls were completely covered with book-laden shelves that ran to the ceiling. Filled with anxiety, he made his way around the main room, staring desperately at the thousands of volumes that surrounded him.

As the asteroid began to flame its way into the atmosphere, he came upon the book at last, and with a great sense of relief, brought the book to the front desk to check it out. Anne was behind the desk, smiling at a stranger. He tried to get her attention, but she did not look his way. He pushed in front of the stranger. There were only moments left. Taking the book without looking at him, Anne stamped the card and handed the book to the stranger, who left the library. Les stood there by the desk, staring at her, appalled now at how perfidious she was.

The windows of the library suddenly flared with a blinding light that jolted him awake as the asteroid struck.

18.

"I TURN OFF HERE," THE driver said, pulling to the side of the highway. "But you don't have far to walk, and the sun's up now." He waited until the hitchhiker got out of the car, and then paused a moment longer, expecting at least a "Thanks for the ride" or a friendly wave goodbye, but the man simply stared back at him.

"Enjoyed our talk," the driver said, trying to be pleasant. "Didn't understand all that chaos stuff and the butterfly bit. But enjoyed it. It kept me awake." He grinned at the man. "Sounds like you're heading for the right place."

The man continued watching him, expressionless, until the driver, seeing he would get no response, shrugged a bit. "Hey, have a good one." He waved goodbye and drove off.

The man watched the car moving away. "An interesting characteristic," he told himself. "Not simply a lesser degree of consciousness. But a willfully maintained ignorance. The concept, after all, is theirs. Dynamical chaos out of small changes in the initial conditions. A butterfly in South America flapping its wings can create a storm in North America."

He stood there quietly for a moment at the side of the highway, looking around at the farm fields and the houses scattered at different distances back from the road. "So many peculiar deficiencies. They struggle to control the forces of their immediate environment by encasing themselves in wood and stone."

He walked along the side of the highway. As he was passing one of the closer farm houses, the front door burst open, and a small boy and a dog came running out. "Hey, Lem! Hey! Hey!" the boy called. Sandy-haired and freckled and full of morning energy, he was dressed in blue-jeans with ragged cuffs and an oversized tee-shirt that hung down almost to his knees. As he raced up the gravel driveway leading to the main road, his dog, a golden retriever puppy, ran excitedly after him, trying to keep up, until the dog saw, ahead by the road, a familiar-looking man in dun-colored shirt and pants. Stopping abruptly, the puppy began to bark loudly at the man, and then started running toward him. "No Lem! No!" the boy yelled. "Don't worry, mister! He won't hurt you! He's just a baby!" The boy now ran after the dog. "Here, Lem! Come!"

The man, standing calmly and watching with growing interest, raised his left hand to the side of his belt. Two elementary levels of consciousness were approaching him in these life forms. "What if I suddenly terminated the electrical impulses moving within the neural networks of their different containments? Would either of them be able to continue functioning?" His curiosity was aroused now. He waited to see whether the dog or the boy would be the first to come into range.

The boy, running faster than the puppy, reached down and scooped him up, stopping a short distance from the man. Nuzzling the puppy as he held it, the boy grinned at the man. "Ain't he something?" He held up the dog. "His name's Lem. Fastest dog in the world. Would you like to pet him?"

The man slowly smiled and then nodded, gesturing for them to come closer, but as the boy started towards him, the puppy gave the boy's cheek a wet lick and then squirmed out of his arms, dropping to the ground and running off, wanting the boy to chase him again. "You crazy dog!" The boy laughed. "Wait for me!" Running happily after the puppy, who headed now toward the house, the boy called back, "Sorry, mister!"

As he watched them retreating, the man's bland features shifted slightly to reveal his disappointment. It would have been an interesting experiment, testing the resiliency of two different containments at such an early stage in their development. There was a notably wide variety of inferior forms existing here, from the fleas that were feeding upon the dog's body, to the dominant inhabitants infesting this planet. Obviously, he did not have the time to examine them all. And yet he recognized, of course, that if he were going to be fair in making his judgment regarding the quality of these life forms, he would need more information. Was his initial impression accurate? He would first have to confirm it scientifically before he took any definite action. And so at this point he would remain, as he always did, open-minded. All possibilities would be objectively considered, even the most ridiculously remote. In spite of all appearances, the life forms here could be evolving in some desirable direction yet to be discovered. "Oh, Fedhisss," he pleasantly mocked himself, "how delightfully ridiculous."

As he walked along the edge of the highway, he looked up at the brightening sky and nodded to himself. "Yes, it is too obvious. Urr will follow my lead and seek for the nearest point of collected information. And so it is only fitting that I prepare some welcome for him. An entertaining moment of controlled chaos. No time, no need, for South America if I intrude much farther up the causal unfolding, well beyond the erratic motions of a butterfly's wings." His eyes brightened with anticipation. "And then the clouds will gather and twist together into that irresistible form of shaped energy feared here on this planet." He smiled as he savored the image.

"And it does raise an interesting possibility. What if Urr's present containment has dulled his awareness, and he actually blunders into the midst of my warning? If it happens, will it dawn on him that I was the one who arranged to have him taken for a spin?

"Pagh! The multiple meanings lurking in these units of sound.

"I hate word play! A disgusting diversion! It could easily become a habit, like a nun's—Pagh!"

19.

LEAVING HIS APARTMENT BY the back steps, Les and Urr paused behind the building to look at the tall elm trees at the rear of the yard. The morning, which had started out unusually calm, with not a single leaf moving in the dry, warm air, was suddenly being transformed into a blustery day, with tree limbs worried back and forth by erratic winds. Storm clouds quickly gathering on the horizon began to tumble out of the west. Small, dark silhouettes of birds winging high above in the sky were tossed around like scraps of paper as they tried to flee from the area.

The back door opened again. Les's landlord came out and joined them in the yard. "Hey!" He looked up at the changing sky. "What happened to the weather report? It was supposed to be nice today." He was a cheerful man in his mid-fifties, with thick black hair that he combed straight back, and the face of a gentle hawk. He was carrying a shotgun cracked open in his left arm, and was wearing a vest filled with tucked-in shotgun shells. On his hip was a holster with a flap of leather closed over a handgun.

"Hello, Mike," Les said. "Say hello to Dr. Urr. He's visiting me for the day." Les pointed to the shotgun. "Looks like you're off to the range again."

Mike shook hands with Urr, who was looking with interest at the two weapons. "Are you a military man?" Urr asked.

Mike grinned. "Used to be. Thirty-some years to a good

pension. Now I can do whatever I want, when I want to do it. It's a great world, isn't it?"

Urr's interest stayed focused on the weapons. "What are you planning to do with them?"

"These?" Mike looked at the weapons as he would two old friends. "Twice a week we meet at the range over near Dunnerton for some skeet shooting"—He held up the shotgun—"and some target practice." He patted the holster. "A little friendly competition." His eyes, which were as black as his hair, glistened with amusement.

"No contest," Les said, smiling. "I bet you blow them all away."

"Not all of them," Mike said modestly. "But I manage to hold my own. And it does keep me off the streets. They're a good bunch of guys. We like to rag each other."

"Why do you do it?" Urr asked.

"Do what" Mike looked at Urr, slightly confused. "Rag the guys?"

"No, I mean why do you continue to shoot your weapons?"

"Oh, that." Mike smiled again and studied Urr a moment. "It's kind of a hobby with me now. I do it because I enjoy it, keeping up the skill. What do you do for enjoyment, Dr. Urr?"

"I travel a great deal," Urr said.

"I did a lot of that when I was on active duty," Mike said. "Maybe too much. Now I think it's great to just take it easy wherever and whenever I want. Ah, the world is too good to me." He glanced at his watch. "Gotta catch my ride. See you guys around." He walked out of the yard and started up the street.

"Mike was a colonel," Les said. "A green beret, with two hitches in Vietnam. He's seen a lot of combat in his life. Quite a man."

"You admire that." Urr watched him, waiting for a response.

Les shrugged slightly. "Sure. Why not? He's a remarkable person. There's no doubt at all that he's a highly trained killer, and yet he's one of the most gentle and caring people I've ever known."

Urr looked out toward the street, but Mike was already out of sight. "Remarkable, indeed," he said. "A compartmentalized killer." He turned back to Les. "How many other kinds will I find here?"

"It's not people like Mike that should worry you, Urr. It's the truly odd ones, the crazies, that are fortunately rarely to be found here. But every society has its share of crazies. As I recall, we're after one now."

"Fedhisss?" Urr considered. "Would I include him among the crazies? If only he were that easy to understand. But the issue he has raised, Les, is a valid one to consider. Who decides what forms of life should exist together in this universe? Your species is making such decisions every day here in your own world. Do not be too quick to dismiss Fedhisss. He is not simply one of your crazies."

They went to Les's car parked by the building. With Urr sitting beside him, Les drove onto the street and made his way out of town. When he turned onto the highway, he headed toward the nearby state university. "It's not too far," he said. "We'll be there in no time."

Urr glanced at him and smiled. "Now that would be quite an accomplishment." As Urr continued looking out the window at the countryside they were driving through, Les tried to view the surroundings from Urr's perspective. On each side of the highway there were plowed fields with different crops growing, and dirt roads running off to farmhouses in the distance. Cutting across the farm lands was a long row of spaced pylons strung with high-tension lines. There was the usual scattering of billboards and road signs. Rte. 208. Milton 27 mi. START YOUR DAY WITH CORNPOPS. Benton's / The Family Restaurant / Meals Served Family Style.

It was a typical hodge-podge of sights that would be seen along any rural highway. Typical. Les smiled. What did that mean to Urr? He reconsidered and saw the common thread running through what they were passing. Crops in the field. Power lines. Packaged food. A restaurant. They all represented in some way energy and its distribution, designed to maintain life. At least the lives of human beings, who had shaped the world to assure their survival. What else could Urr possibly expect to see?

The car was suddenly rocked by a powerful gust of wind that almost sent it off the edge of the highway. "Whoa!" Les said, gripping the steering wheel harder. The clouds had tumbled overhead, darkening the sky. Lightning flashes began to strike in the distance. "That's some storm we've got brewing. I hope we can reach the university before it hits."

Urr began to watch the sky closely. "I do not like this."

"Don't worry," Les said. "These summer storms are often fast and furious. It will probably leave just as quickly as it came."

Urr was now concentrating on the highway far ahead. "There!" he said. "That dirt road coming up!"

"What about it?" Les said, puzzled by Urr's tone of voice.

"Turn off on that road," Urr said, "and drive away from the highway."

"Why?" Les said, slowing the car and pulling to a stop.

"No, Les! Do as I said! Quickly now!"

Confused by Urr's behavior, Les hesitated, looking to him for some explanation.

"Please!" Urr appealed. "Quickly! It's important!"

"Okay," Les said, still puzzled. He shifted gears and shot ahead, turning onto the dirt road and speeding away from the highway. Behind the car the wind was whipping around the dust that billowed up. "How far do you want me to go?"

When they had reached some distance away from the

highway, Urr said, "Here. Stop here, and turn the car around. We'll watch from here."

"Watch what?" Les said. He had trouble turning the car on the narrow road, but finally got it pointed back toward the highway.

"What are we looking for?" Les said, peering out through the dust they had raised.

"That," Urr said, and he pointed up the highway.

Les felt himself stagger back against the car seat. "I don't believe it! A twister! It's a tornado!" he said turning to Urr as though he needed to explain the sight. "There's never been a tornado in this area!"

The clouds had lowered ominously, and the funnel shape, which had touched down onto the highway, was moving in their direction with the increasing roar of an oncoming freight-train. "God! I'd better get back farther!"

"No need to," Urr said. "It will stay on the highway."

As he had predicted, the twister was making its way directly along the highway, sending most of the cars and trucks in sight veering crazily out of its path into the fields on both sides. The tornado appeared to be focusing its intensity on clearing the road, lifting the few cars that stayed on the road and flinging them aside, like a child in a tantrum throwing toys. A trailer-truck, loaded with soft-drinks, was lifted straight up from the road and spun like a top. Its back doors popped open, sending cases and bottles of soda spiraling out like a lawn sprinkler, until the truck came crashing back to the ground with the screeching sound of twisting metal. The tornado continued on its way in a straight path up the highway, never leaving the road until, in the distance, the funnel shape finally broke up and disappeared.

"My God!" Les said, stunned by the sight. "I tell you, it's never happened here! What kind of a freak storm—" He turned to Urr and saw the look on his face. "Oh, no," Les said. "Not Fedhisss. Don't try to tell me it's Fedhisss. How could he create a tornado, for God's sake?" He looked back to the highway. "We've got to get out there to help. The people in those cars and that truck, we've got to help them." He reached for the shift.

"Listen," Urr said, gripping Les by the arm to steady him. "If you take a moment to look, you'll see that people are already there to help."

It was true. Those vehicles that had managed to pull off the road in time were spewing out people who were running back to the highway, gathering around each of the damaged vehicles. "We have something much more urgent to do. We know now for certain that Fedhisss has come this way, that he, too, is heading for your university. He is likely already there. If we do not stop him soon, whatever he has done here will be of little importance."

Les could feel his anger rising. "Damn it, if he's that dangerous, you're the one who has to stop him. He's your responsibility. Do something about it!" He winced at the direction his thoughts were taking him. "Can't you understand? It's not our fight. Just go somewhere else. The middle of the Atlantic Ocean! Then when he tries to stop you, nobody else will get hurt."

"If that would help," Urr said, "I would be pleased to do it. But, unfortunately, his vehicle has landed near your town, and he knows that I have followed him here. He will act at some point today to terminate my pursuit, before we reach the time that our vehicles signal their locations."

"But what if he decides to leave early?" Les said, sensing the false hope he was trying to stir up. "He could make a run for it and get far enough away so that you couldn't follow him."

"I would know the moment he activated his vehicle," Urr

said, "and I would return as quickly as I could to mine. That would simply prolong the pursuit. This time I believe that Fedhisss will prefer to be more decisive, for he understands that he has the advantage here. By now he will have recognized the peculiarly destructive nature of your species. Making his way among you, he will assume that he can quickly find the materials that he will need to stop me from pursuing him." He paused a moment to study Les, as though unsure if he were communicating adequately with him. "And he will also be gathering information, Les. Have I conveyed that point to you clearly enough? Fedhisss intends, while he is here, to find the answer to a question of central concern to him. Are you worthy of existence in his universe?"

"Good Lord," Les said, despairingly.

"He's chosen your university to satisfy those needs." Urr continued watching him closely. "What is he going to find there, Les, that will allow him to stop me and to condemn you?"

Les considered the question, but nothing came to mind. There was no military or industrial research going on there, nothing he could think of that would pose any danger. And the information that would be available? It was an accumulation of the best that humankind had achieved, in the sciences and the humanities. How could anyone turn that against humanity?

"I believe," Urr said, when Les didn't respond, "that I had better see for myself." He released his hold on Les's arm. "We should proceed now without any further delay."

Les could hear a siren in the distance. He saw an ambulance making its way slowly along the highway among the scattered vehicles, as though uncertain of where to stop first. Still struggling to calm himself as he put the car into gear, he drove back over the dirt road. As he turned onto the highway, he shook his head in exasperation at an obvious oversight that occurred to him. "You haven't even described him to me yet. When we get there, how will I know if I see him?"

"That part is easy," Urr said. "The energy infusion process in our vehicles is identical."

"So?" Les said, glancing at him.

Urr turned his face to Les. "So Fedhisss will look exactly like me."

20.

THE STATE UNIVERSITY CAMPUS was a sprawling collection of brick buildings, monuments to the growth of the university from its founding in the early 1900s, and to its long-standing commitment to lead the way in the advancement of knowledge. They drove slowly through the campus, eying everyone in sight. Students and staff were entering and departing the buildings, making their ways along the sidewalks, gathering in small groups on the lawns. Some of the groups had formed around anyone with a portable radio, apparently listening to the latest news about the tornado touching down in the area.

"It stays pretty busy here in the summer," Les said. "We run a good number of programs." He glanced at Urr. "Do you think we'll see him—or see another you, I mean—just strolling around the campus?"

"I do not believe so," Urr said. "Fedhiss will be after specific information and materials. Most likely in that order. What are these buildings around us?"

"Over there," Les said, pointing through the windshield, "is where most humanities courses are offered—which reminds me." He looked at his watch. "I have a class coming up. I'll have to meet them, if only to excuse the class. Next to it is the theater. Then along here in a row are the Student Union, Criminal Justice, the Health Sciences, Engineering. Up ahead there is our new Science and Technology Center."

Urr looked curiously at Les. "And this building here to the right of us?"

Les paused a moment before answering, as though something off to the left had caught his attention. "Oh, that," he said. "The library. You can see it's a rather extensive campus. If Fedhisss is here, he could be anywhere. Where would you like to start?"

"I believe," Urr said, "I would like to start at the library."

"Why there?" Les said, frowning.

"Information first," Urr answered. "Then materials."

"What kind of information?"

"The answer to another question."

Les had slowed the car as they approached the street that ran beside the library. "What question?"

"I need to know," Urr said, "why it is possible for human beings to kill each other."

Les had stopped the car at the intersection. He sat there, considering the question. "There have to be a hundred reasons," he said. "Hatred, greed, fear, revenge, political power, you name it."

Urr shook his head slowly. "I am not looking for sociological reasonings. I need to know more about the depths of human nature, what has evolved there and still exists that makes such a peculiarly destructive act possible." He turned to study Les again. "Human beings throughout your world have apparently become so accustomed to killing each other that they assume it must be a natural, if not a necessary, part of human existence. I would like to know if that is true."

Les returned Urr's searching look. "That's one hell of a question," he said. "And you think you can find the answer here?"

"Possibly," Urr said. "But I will need to spend some time in the library. Could I do so, perhaps as you teach your class?"

A car behind them beeped its horn. Les glanced in the

rearview mirror and saw that he was holding up traffic. "Yes, of course," he said, and he turned the corner, making his way along the street to park behind the library. As he pulled into the lot, a nearby car was backing out. "We're in luck. This lot is usually crammed full. Parking is always a problem here."

As Les pulled into the space, Urr continued watching him, as though there were something new in Les that had caught Urr's interest. "I will not be familiar with how the knowledge accumulated here has been organized. Is there anyone in the library you know who could be of help to me?"

When they both got out of the car, Les stood a moment in the lot, looking at the rear of the building as though reluctant to enter. "The reference librarian," he said, clearly troubled. "I'll introduce you and then go on to my class."

They went into the building, up a short flight of stairs, and then into a large reading room, where students, scattered among the long rectangular tables, were silently reading or taking notes. Making their way across the room and out a double door, they reached the main entrance area, where the check-out counter was staffed by a red-headed woman in her forties. "Well," the woman said in a throaty voice when she saw Les. "Look what the wind blew in!" Her face had a florid, inviting warmth, with firm features that were just beginning to soften, like the flesh of a ripened peach. "Took a tornado to get you back here, did it, Dr. Marks?"

A young woman seated at a desk off to one side looked up and saw Les. On her desk was a name-plate almost hidden under materials stacked around it—*Anne Sommers, Reference Librarian*. She stood up, smiling hesitantly, and came to the counter. "Hello, Les." Her voice was soft, barely audible, her eyes large and deep brown above high cheekbones, a classic look of beauty in a face unsure of itself. She stood silently then, watching Les, waiting to see if he would acknowledge her presence.

"Hello, Anne." He did not return her look. He frowned and stared down at the counter, as though trying to keep something important in mind, not wanting to be distracted.

Urr stood beside him, watching the exchange with intense interest.

"I have a favor to ask," Les said. "This is Dr. Urr, from out of state. He's researching a subject and could use your help."

Anne held out her hand. "Welcome to the university, Dr. Urr. I'd be pleased to help in any way I could."

"That would be very good of you," Urr said, as he shook her hand and held her gaze a moment.

"Manners, manners, Dr. Marks," the red-headed woman said, focusing her smile on Urr. "Aren't you going to introduce me to your charming friend?"

"Sorry, Millie," Les said. "Dr. Urr, this is Millie Watson. She's a whiz at keeping the library a quiet place to study."

"As quiet as a grave," Millie whispered, widening her eyes.

"The grave's a fine and private place," Urr said, quoting from the Marvell poem he had gathered earlier from Les.

"But none, I think, do there embrace," Millie said. "The story of my life." She leaned forward to take Urr's hand, pulling him slightly toward her with a warm and inviting look. "Hi," she said, slowly breathing out the word as she kept his hand in hers.

Urr was apparently surprised by the feeling that spread through him from his physical contact with this woman. "My pleasure," he said, smiling widely.

"Ah," said Millie, holding his look. "Pleasure." She spoke the word as though it were a promise she was making Urr of things to come.

"Dr. Urr," Anne said, "may I ask what subject you are interested in?"

Urr turned somewhat reluctantly away from Millie to answer. "I have rather wide-ranging interests, Miss Sommers.

At the moment I need to focus on astronomy, physics, chemistry, and the emergence and evolution of life here on earth."

"Well, that narrows it down!" Millie said, laughing. "But Anne here is your girl, Dr. Urr. She'll have you surrounded with books in no time."

"In no time," Urr repeated, remembering the phrase. "Now that would be truly helpful."

"I'll be off to my class then," Les said, glancing at his watch. "Let's say in about an hour I'll check back with you here. That should give you plenty of time to find your answer." He shook his head in disbelief and walked away. "Take good care of that man," he said, waving without looking back.

"My favorite activity," Millie said, with a throaty laugh, as her eyes took in Urr.

Anne continued to watch Les until he went out the front door. And then she stood for a few moments looking at the door, as though Les were still framed in it. Finally, she turned and gave her full attention to Urr. "Where would you like to start?" she said. She had an exceptionally good memory that served her well in her profession, but she could not remember where she had seen Dr. Urr before, and she was sure that she had.

"You're very kind to give me your time," Urr said. He returned her look for a moment. "Perhaps I could do something for you in return."

"Oh?" Anne said, wondering what he meant.

21.

HERE, ON THIS REPUGNANT planet (Pagh! I hate alliteration!), human beings, the dominant life form, consider themselves to be the center of their universe, watched over with tender loving care by the creator of their universe, who hangs around to keep in touch with every single one of these beings so that he can listen to their pathetically self-centered voices and grant their whining wishes (Pagh!). I will admit to being amused by their astonishing arrogance, their bloated sense of self-importance, their assumption that they are the primary concern, the central focus, the darling, of some creator who has cobbled together this endless universe, a creator who either treats them well or punishes them according to some divine plan that always remains just beyond their capacity to know. Oh, the agility of idiocy!

And on the other end of the see-saw sit their scientists, who say that they are finally about to discover a theory that will explain everything, a rationally arrived at understanding of the workings of the universe in all of its mechanic glory. No need for a god here. The scientist is ready to fill that role. Just give them a little more time, and they will be able to control the universe to everyone's heart's content. Did they not find the atom, the basic building-block of matter? Nothing smaller. No doubt about it. But wait a minute. The atom has structure! Protons, and neutrons, and electrons. The basic building-blocks of matter. Nothing smaller. No doubt about it. But wait a minute. Protons and neutrons have structure! Quarks of various odd labels. The basic building-blocks of matter. Nothing smaller. No doubt about it. But wait a minute....

And each end of the see-saw, as it rises, pauses a moment at the top to look disdainfully down upon the other, for each end believes that only its view of their little playground is the pre-eminent one. Up and down. Up and down.

How should I judge these beings and their silly beliefs?

Objectively, of course.

22.

"WE'RE VERY PROUD OF our new Science and Technology Center," Professor Enders said. "State of the art. Everything you could hope for."

"Everything I could hope for," Fedhisss said, and his eyes gleamed with anticipated pleasure as they entered one of the technology labs. Small groups and single students were pursuing projects at different stations in front of two banks of computers running through the room. But what immediately caught Fedhisss's eye was the large stock of electronic parts and equipment in the cabinets and on the shelves covering the walls of the room.

"An abbreviated tour, but I hope it has been of some help," Professor Enders said. "I have a meeting now I must hasten to, so you will have to excuse me."

"You have no idea of how helpful you have been," Fedhisss said, shaking the professor's hand and then walking with him out into the hall as though he, too, were leaving. When the professor turned the corridor and was out of sight, Fedhisss returned to the lab and began to explore the range of materials that were stored there, occasionally taking down specific parts, as though he were making his way through an electronic supermarket. Those students who paid him any attention, having seen him with Professor Enders, assumed that he belonged there and went back to concentrating on their work.

When Fedhisss had gathered a fairly large selection of

parts, he carried them to one of the work tables, where electrical outlets and soldering guns were available. Sitting down, he began to assemble the parts.

He was watched with some interest by one of the nearby students, a young man with shaggy hair and an earring, and a t-shirt that was stenciled *Ready to plug in*.

The student came over and stood behind Fedhisss. "Hi," he said. "What's that you're making?"

Fedhisss turned and looked at him, expressionless, until something appeared to catch his interest. "You have advanced electronic skills."

"So they say." The student smiled and tried to look around Fedhisss at what was on the work table. "You, too?"

"Me, too," Fedhisss said.

"Into something interesting?" the student asked.

"Very," Fedhisss said.

"Commercial possibilities?" The student's interest seemed to sharpen.

Fedhisss thought a moment. "Not commercial," he said. "Disruptive."

"Disruptive?" the student said, trying to put the term into some meaningful context. "Just what is it you're making?"

"A shattering device," Fedhisss said.

"You putting me on, man?" The student's voice took on an edge.

"Not at all," Fedhisss said. "You asked, and I told you."

"All right, what's a shattering device?"

Fedhisss looked down at his work. "Obviously, a device for shattering things."

"What things?" the student said. "What are you going to shatter?"

The question appeared to delight Fedhisss. He turned and beamed at the student. "People! I'm going to shatter people! Isn't that a wonderful idea?"

"Yeah, sure," the student said, disgusted now for having wasted his time on some asshole trying to pull his leg. He went back to his computer.

"Stay around," Fedhisss said to him, "and you can have the honor of being the first one I will shatter."

"Forget it," the student said, focusing his attention on the computer screen before him. "I've got more important things to do."

"So have I," Fedhisss said. "May we both succeed."

"Sure." The student was barely paying attention to him now. "Go for it, man."

"I believe I will," Fedhisss said.

23.

ANNE HAD FOUND A seat for Urr at a staff table in a small office where he would not be disturbed. As they had made their way to the office, passing through a section of the library's extensive stacks and then on through the main reference room, Urr had trailed behind her, trying to take in everything he saw to determine the size of the task he was about to attempt.

"How long can you spend with us today, Dr. Urr?" Les had asked for her help, and she wanted to respond as fully as she could.

"Oh," Urr said, smiling pleasantly at her, "at least an hour."

She returned the smile, somewhat shyly, assuming that he was joking with her. "Well," she said, "then we had better get to work."

"Could we start," Urr said, "with two basic texts, one in physics and one in astronomy? I would like to know what scientists currently believe about the evolution of the physical matter that has resulted in the formation of this planet."

"Well," Anne said, her eyes widening at the thought of the subject, "there would be a good number of basic texts in each of those fields. I'll pick out one from a publishing house that specializes in the area, and you can tell me if it meets your needs." She left the office.

In a few minutes she returned, carrying a large book. "This one has a good reputation," she said. "A well-known introductory text in physics, but I've been told that it can also take you to an advanced level in the field." She placed it before him on the table, smiling somewhat sympathetically. "It's almost a thousand pages, though. That, by itself, could use up most of your hour."

Urr liked the smile she gave him, the gift of a gentle person, tentative, a soft appeal, wanting to be liked. He tried to think of a single word that might describe her nature, a word that would accurately distinguish her particular character, and it finally came to him. She was, he realized, harmless. Across the spectrum of life forms and among the variety of human beings that he had found on this troubling planet, that was high praise, indeed. She was one of this world's hidden treasures.

Anne left him with the physics text and went off again to find one in astronomy. When she returned, she stopped suddenly in the doorway and stood there, completely still, as she watched what he was doing. With a carefully controlled motion, he was riffling the pages of large sections of the physics book as he held some kind of tiny device above them. Within a few moments, he had made his way through the book. Glancing up, he saw the puzzled look on her face.

He turned up the palm of his hand to show her the tiny device. "It's an advanced model of what you might call a scanner," he said. "It converts your printed materials into an electronic form that will make them much more expediently accessible to me."

"Are you telling me," Anne said, coming to the table to peer more closely at the device, "that you have just scanned the entire contents of the physics text that quickly, and into something that small?"

"Is that difficult for you to believe?" he said. He considered her a moment. "Then I will make a trade with you. Would it be accurate to say that across your life you have mentally accumulated a considerable amount of printed materials?"

"Do you mean," Anne said, frowning, "have I read a great deal? I've always enjoy reading, since I was a very small child, so, yes, you could say that I've read a fair amount."

"Well, then," Urr said, "since I will obviously not have enough time to learn what I need if I proceed at this pace, and since your background would be of considerable use to help me move ahead more quickly, I will trade you the contents of the physics book for what you have read."

"I don't understand," Anne said. "How could we possibly make such a trade?"

"Are you agreeable?" Urr said. "I believe that you will find it an interesting experience."

She studied him a moment, wondering if she should take him seriously. Les had apparently wanted to help him. How much did he know about this man? And where had she seen him before? The question kept nagging her. With a tentative smile and a slight shrug, she stood quietly by the table in the small office, waiting to see what he would do next.

Urr stood and came around the table to stand in front of her. Opening his hands to show her that all he had in them was the tiny device, he held her gaze as he lifted the hand with the device in it up to one side of her head. She stiffened a bit as he reached out and made contact, but held herself in place. Urr then lifted his other hand and touched the opposite side of her head.

She jerked a bit, with a startled look, her eyes wide with surprise, then confusion, then a tinge of fear. "What did you.... I don't...." And then her attention was drawn inward. She stood there, her eyes now slightly averted, and slowly recognized what had occurred within her. "The physics text," she said, looking now at Urr. "I've read it." She stared at him in disbelief.

Urr returned her look, but with a sadness that had entered his face. "I do not yet understand what evolutionary role is fulfilled through such deep experiences of grief. You were at such a young age. It must have been exceedingly painful for you to find her that way."

"What do you mean?" Anne said, her thoughts in confusion. And then, with a shock, she realized what he did mean. "How could you possibly know? I've never told...not even Les...." Unable to look away from Urr, she struggled to regain control of herself. "Who are you?" She continued staring at him, her mind in a turmoil, until another and much more frightening question surfaced. "What are you?"

He offered her a sympathetic face. "Just another human being."

24.

A HUMAN BEING IS an awkward ordering of matter shaped by a purposeless evolutionary process into a highly vulnerable accumulation of diversified cells. The cells have combined with or harbor a number of other symbiotic life forms, all cobbled together into a temporary containment of consciousness. These beings assume, without question, that they are representative of some pinnacle of evolutionary development, a special order of physical existence that can slough off the remains of their decomposing bodies like borrowed clothes and rise up into the sky above their mortal world to a never-ending existence of happiness and pleasure. Isn't that remarkable!

There is only one conclusion to be reached. Objectively. Inescapably. The cells that have accumulated to contain that twisted consciousness need to be uncoupled again. And the method I will use to achieve that goal? It will prove to be an interesting experiment. If I place a negative charge on each living cell—brilliant! the simplicity of it!—it will cause them to repel each other. And if all their cells repel each other instantaneously, then I will be able to see them *shatter*.

Yes, an extensive shattering of their corporeal bodies. Above each of their towns, a mushroom cloud of repellant cells will arise and blossom, to be blown about and carried off by the fickle winds. Their misty bodies will finally be uplifted to the heavens. And their windy souls at last will be released from their cells.

When they see the devastation that I am wreaking upon them, how will they react to it? What has always been their response to every incomprehensible source of destruction they have experienced?

They will deify it, and bow down before it, and seek its forgiveness.

And then, for the brief time they have left, they will begin to worship me.

I am not averse to their doing so.

25.

Walking down the hallway past a row of biology department faculty offices, Fedhisss was carrying a metallic box about the size of a small suitcase. His right hand held what appeared to be a camera. He was heading for a biology laboratory that he had been told was at the end of the hallway. The laboratory, which focused on the study of language abilities in primates, contained a well-known chimpanzee named Bingo whose sign-language vocabulary was nearing three hundred words.

Reaching the laboratory, Fedhisss looked through the glass paneling in the door. There was only one person inside, young enough to be a student lab assistant, who was sweeping the floor around a large cage that held the chimp. As Fedhisss entered, the student turned with a questioning look. "Can I help you?" He was small and slightly stooped over, with unkempt hair and beard, giving the impression that he was on the wrong side of the cage bars.

"Yes," said Fedhisss. "Professor Enders sent me. He thought there would be no objection to my taking a picture of your famous resident here." The chimp had come to the front of the cage. Holding the bars, it shook them slightly and made a few high sounds. Its eyes, so close to being human in their expressiveness, were watching Fedhisss with a mild interest.

"Our star border," the student said, as he reached out and brushed his fingers across one of Bingo's hands on the bars.

Bingo pulled the hand away and began to make three quick gestures with it, over and over again.

"What is he doing?" Fedhisss said.

"He's signing," the student said, smiling through his beard at the chimp. "Bingo...want...banana." The student repeated the gestures. "Bingo *always* want banana." He put his face close to the cage and shook his head. "Noooooo."

The chimp shook the bars harder and began to make screeching sounds of protest.

"Behave yourself, Bingo," the student said. "You have company." He turned back to Fedhisss. "Professor Jurgens doesn't usually allow anyone but staff in here. Bingo is his pride and joy. His baby, really. A member of his family. He's been working with him for years. If something was to happen to Bingo, I think the Professor would really flip out. Over the edge." He motioned with his hand as though it was diving off a cliff. "But since Professor Enders has sent you, hey, why not? A quick shot or two. He's all yours."

"Thank you," Fedhisss said. He set the large metallic box that he was carrying on the floor and raised the object that looked like a camera up before his face. Looking through the camera at the chimp in the cage, he made a number of adjustments and then got ready to shoot. Lowering the camera again, he turned to the student. "Would you mind standing there right next to the cage? I'd like to include you in the picture."

"Sure," the student said, looking pleased. "What's the picture for, anyways?"

"It's a test shot, really," Fedhisss said, "to see how my device works. This," he held up the camera, "is a smaller model of that." He pointed to the metallic box on the floor.

"What's it supposed to do?" the student said, as he took his place beside the cage and made a few grunting noises in at

Bingo, who had begun to shake his bars again. People had taken his picture before, and it was always followed by a reward.

"We'll know in a moment," Fedhisss said, as he sighted through the device.

The student stiffened into a pose. Bingo put his face between the bars and opened his lips wide, protruding his teeth in a simian smile that always got a good response from his viewers.

"Any last words?" Fedhisss said, having framed them both in the device. He could feel his excitement peaking, and he wanted to prolong the pleasure, but the urge to see the result became overwhelming.

"You mean," said the student, "like 'Say cheeeeeeese!'"

As the sound of the prolonged vowel came to him, Fedhisss clicked a lever on the side of the camera and heard the sound replaced by a whoosh. Instantaneously, student and chimp exploded into a damp mist. The substance flew against the walls of the cage and out through the bars to mingle with the mist that was rapidly expanding from the spot where the student had been standing, marked now by where the student's clothes had collapsed into a pile on the floor. Fedhisss, overcome with delight, kept stepping backwards, trying to stay beyond the range of the misty substance as it spread out through the laboratory. He did not see the man who had entered the laboratory behind him until he had actually bumped into him. Turning, he saw the man's face staring around the room with a barely controlled anger, and then coming to focus on Fedhisss.

"What the hell is going on here?" Professor Jurgens said.

26.

IN THE FINAL MINUTES of the class hour, Les looked out at the roomful of faces that were obviously waiting somewhat impatiently now for him to dismiss the class. It had not been a good meeting. He was simply too distracted, and the class was apparently aware of it, for their meetings before had always resulted in lively discussions that often spilled over beyond the end of class. Across most of the summer session, they had been discussing the concepts of fate and free will as illustrated through the lives of famous characters in literature. Were they ultimately free to choose and so responsible for their own acts, or were there powers beyond their control that determined their destinies?

"For our next meeting," Les told them, "I want you to focus on the final three chapters. Throughout the book, Melville has been exploring the central question of whether free will, fate, or chance brings about the events that occur within this world. In the Loom of Time chapter he has Ishmael tell us that all three somehow interweave together to do so. But beyond that point, as we now approach the end of the novel, all we have so far is Ishmael's statement that they do. In the final three chapters, however, you will discover one of the most remarkable accomplishments in literature, for in the closing and decisive conflict between Ahab and Moby-Dick, Melville will now dramatize for us, he will actually allow us to experience for ourselves, that free will, fate, and chance all interweavingly do work together to bring about the concluding events of the book. Keep the loom firmly in mind as you read, and you will undergo one of this world's most unforgettable literary experiences."

As he said the phrase "one of this world's," he clutched for a moment, unable to speak further. Looking out at the roomful of students watching him, waiting to hear what he would say next, he wondered how they would respond if he told them what was distracting him. The thought of doing so made him smile slightly. "Free will or fate?" he said, posing the question as much to himself as to them. "And what of chance? If we had enough knowledge, would we be able to take our lives within our own hands and mold them into whatever shape we chose? Or will our lives always be predominantly within the grip of forces beyond our control?" He saw that he had caught their attention again, and he lowered his voice, leaning slightly forward, as though he were about to share with them a troublesome truth. "I can say to you now that you will likely not have very long to wait for the answer." He felt the growing urge to tell them. "It may happen more quickly than you could possibly realize"—But what kind of irrational idiot would he sound like?— "as you sit here at this relatively calm moment"—Someone who had lost it, gone over the edge!— "listening to me babble on. Enough. I'll see you next time."

Les hurried from the room before any of the students could speak to him. As he left the building, his sense of urgency welled up again within him, and he strode along as quickly as he could, barely holding himself back from breaking into a run. What was going on back at the library? And where was Fedhisss? He glanced compulsively at everyone he passed, prepared to be startled by seeing another Urr. What would he do if he saw Fedhisss and Urr wasn't with him? What would Fedhisss do if he knew he had been seen? Les felt the darkening sole of a foot descending upon him.

27.

As Les entered the main entrance of the library, Anne stood up quickly from her desk and came around toward him. He could see the strained look on her face. She took him by the arm and led him over to a quiet corner, her eyes full of anguish. "Who is he, Les?" She was almost whispering. "Who have you brought here? What is he doing here?"

His stomach knotted at the thought that Urr had revealed his identity to her. Urr had no right to involve her in this. "Did he do something to upset you, damn him?" He glance around. "Where is he now?"

"In that small staff office next to the reference room."

She came closer to him, and he could feel the warmth of her body almost making contact with his.

"What's wrong, Les?" She looked up at him, her face showing the distress that she was feeling. "Why won't you tell me?" Her eyes, pleading for an answer, grew moist. "You've been avoiding me. I don't know why. Have I done something to displease you?"

He froze for a moment as he looked at her face, so gentle in its loveliness. The pain he saw there twisted his heart, and he could feel his own eyes moistening as he reached out and took her in his arms, every part of him drawn to her, desperately wanting her—until he felt the old resistance rising within him. "Oh, God, Anne, I'm so confused." He held her tighter, not wanting to let go, as though he could squeeze the feeling away. But it loosened his grip, and he finally stepped back, keeping her at arm's length. "Tell me what happened with Dr. Urr."

The pleasure she had felt as he held her close waned quickly as her thoughts returned to the upsetting incident in the small staff office. "I'm not sure I can describe it, Les." She groped again for some explanation. "He took the contents of a large physics text, and he gave it to me. I mean, he put it into my mind, as though I had actually read the book." She watched him expectantly, waiting for him to respond. But he said nothing, holding her gaze until she continued. "And then," she lowered her eyes, "I don't know how, but he knew things about me, things about my childhood that I've never told anyone." She closed her arms around herself, as though a chill had passed through her. "It was a frightening experience, Les. Who is that man? How can he do things like that?"

Les felt his tension ease somewhat. Urr's identity was still hidden. Anne had not been drawn into their search for Fedhisss. "I'll tell you soon, Anne, I promise," he said. "Although I don't see how you'll ever be able to believe me. Dr. Urr is trying to do something important, and he says he needs my help to do it, and, well, I think I should give it to him. But there's no time now to explain. Do you know if he's still in the office?"

"It's where I left him," Anne said.

"Then will you trust me, and let me work this thing out? It should all be over by this evening." One way or the other, he thought to himself.

Her voice was soft, her look offering him so much more than just her trust. "All right," she said, and she raised her hand to touch his cheek, wanting again to make contact with him. But he stepped back abruptly as her hand approached, still under the influence of his own confusing feelings, and so she dropped it and smiled sadly at him across the protective distance he had opened again around himself.

Urr was still in the small office when Les reached it. He was sitting next to a pile of additional books that he had gathered for himself from the stacks in the library.

Les stopped in the doorway, trying to keep his voice under control. "I want you to leave Anne, Miss Sommers, out of this. I do not want you tampering in any way with her. Do you understand?"

Urr looked up, his eyebrown raised. "Did I do something wrong?"

"Just leave her out of this," Les said.

Urr considered him a moment. "I needed her background in the organization and storage of the information that has been accumulated here. But I did not have time, Les, to work with her. Gathering that background from her has allowed me not only to proceed more quickly with my search, but to have no further need of contact with her. I thought that would be what you preferred. Was I wrong?"

"The end may have been right," Les said, "but the means were too upsetting to her." He sensed the weakness of his complaint, which irritated him further. "Just leave her alone."

"As you wish," Urr said, nodding. "It is an interesting lesson you have been teaching me about yourself, Les, and your relation to Miss Sommers, something not presented at all clearly within these books." He gestured at the stack on the table.

"What do you mean?" Les said, and he quickly regretted asking the question, for they were getting too close to a subject that he preferred to avoid.

"The complicated fluidity of your emotions," Urr said. "The contradictory and conflicting forces of those emotions, which can buffet you so unexpectedly back and forth, like the erratic winds of a storm. For someone who has worked as hard as you have to live within the sheltering limits of your own reasoning mind, it must be an exceedingly uncomfortable state in which to exist. Do you not find it so?"

"What I find right now," Les said, wanting to change the subject, "is the need for you to stop Fedhisss from doing any more harm. He could make his move at any time, Urr. Here on campus, or when we're back in town. Think of how many people"—he struggled with the wave of despair that washed through him. "You need to stop him now, before he acts."

"Does Miss Sommers live in town?" Urr asked.

"Yes, damn it. But let's leave her out of this. It's Fedhisss you're after. What about him?" He pointed to the books on the table. "Have you found anything helpful?"

"Yes, but it's taking too much time. I need a more expedient access. How well do you know the other people teaching here?"

"I've been here a number of years," Les said, "so I know most faculty reasonably well."

"Is there a physicist here that you know?"

"Yes. Professor Lichte."

"Can you find him quickly?"

"I think so," Les said. Urr stood up then, and they left the office.

As they went across the main entrance area, past the check-out counter, Millie Watson came around to meet Les and linked her arm in his, pulling him close as they walked along. "If you and Anne want to steam up the windows in here, I would recommend a more private place." She grinned at him and then at Urr, her face flushed with pleasure.

Les frowned and shook his head. "Not now, Millie." He freed his arm from her grip and kept walking.

"Oooh," Millie said. "A shift in the wind." She put her

finger in her mouth, and, as she looked at Urr, slowly drew it out, and then held it up. "Could be a storm ahead. Be careful, Dr. Urr."

Urr smiled, "I will, Miss Watson," and then turned to Les. "You see?" But Les did not return his look. "Contradictory forces within you?" Urr considered. "Or erratic winds blowing through you? Which do you think better describes it?"

Les hurried out the door, leaving the question behind.

28.

As I CONTINUE MY pursuit of Fedhisss, I am gathering a considerable mass of knowledge formally accumulated by human beings. I find, however, that the accumulation is a problem in itself, for, rather than a mass, it is more a mess of conflicting intellectual concepts and psychically comforting conclusions. This mess, strange to say, is persistently maintained by the mature members of the planet, who infuse it into the younger members of each generation. Thus, each of their young, born as an irrational being, is raised in a world constructed out of other people's often erroneous thoughts and misplaced emotions.

During their waking days, they often yearn to rise above the vulnerability of their physical containments. But in the night they remain fearful of breaking their bonds to the material world. To illustrate this quandary persisting within them, I have selected the following example of how they occasionally shape their language to intensify their thoughts. It also shows that they possess at least a glimmering of their predicament.

GROUNDLING

As sleep approached, I raised my hand
Against the coming night,
And saw my fingers, silhouetted
By the starry light,
Slowly turn to radiant feathers,

Wavering and white.

Above the darkness of my bed,
The moon, with eager eye,
Was whispering that I could pass
Beyond him as I fly,
To ride upon the wind that blows
The stars across the sky.

I whispered back, "Who understands
The mumblings of the moon?"
And heard, from out across the lake,
The calling of a loon.
I hid my head, and curled to sleep
Within a dark cocoon.
There is a fear much worse than fear
Of falling from a height.
It haunts me like a specter hovering
Over me at night—
A silhouette of empty fingers,
Under starry light.

Human beings are paradoxical creatures, with intellects struggling to emerge out of a weltering of underlying emotions yet to be harmonized within them, leaving them incomplete and unpredictable. Will that prove to be an impediment to Fedhisss? Or will he have little difficulty in shaping them to his own ends?

29.

"Who are you?" Professor Jurgens glared at him. "This lab is off-limits to visitors. What are you doing in here?"

Fedhisss smiled politely. "Professor Enders thought that you would have no objections to my taking a quick picture of your famous chimp. I had no intention of intruding on you. If you wish, I'll leave immediately." He reached down for the metal box that he had set on the floor.

"Enders? He sent you?" Professor Jurgens' anger receded a bit. "No, I would have no objections if he has sent you." He looked at the cage. "But where the hell is Bingo? If that little toad of a student has taken him out again, I'll wring his damned neck." He glanced around and grimaced. "And what the hell is this sticky mess? What's been going on here?"

"I understand that you're very deeply and emotionally attached to Bingo." Fedhisss was watching him with a new interest.

"You could say that," Professor Jurgens said somewhat gruffly.

"And if anything was to happen to Bingo, it would be very upsetting to you." Fedhisss considered him a moment. "How upsetting?"

"What do you mean? What are you getting at?" Professor Jurgens said, his voice rising with concern. "Has something happened to Bingo? Do you know where he is?"

"I can show you exactly what happened to him," Fedhisss said. He was curious now. They were such a peculiar life form, harboring the capacity to destroy each other. What

93

did it take to bring it out?

Like a rattler striking, Fedhisss reached out and, before Professor Jurgens could move, tapped him on the side of the head. Fedhisss then backstepped to put some distance between them.

"What—" Professor Jurgens looked startled, his eyes widening as he stared at Fedhisss. Then his face darkened as he retreated inside himself. He stood there, transfixed, as he watched the unfolding of what had taken place in the laboratory earlier. As the chimp suddenly disintegrated in its cage, spraying out between the bars, Professor Jurgens let out a pained howl of protest, an extended wail of grief and anger that was slowly stifled as his throat constricted and he began to grasp for air. The event finally faded within him, and like a half-drowned man, he struggled mentally back to the surface to stare again, in disbelief, at Fedhisss.

"The sticky stuff," Fedhisss said, gesturing around the room. "It's Bingo and your student." He smiled gleefully. "Isn't that remarkable?"

Professor Jurgens looked at the film of greasy material that was still dripping down the bars of the cage, and the truth of what Fedhisss had shown him finally sank in. "My God, who are you? What kind of insane mind..." His disbelief quickly turned to an uncontrollable anger. "You son-of-a-bitch!" He was a large man, with meaty hands that tightened now into heavy fists. He raised them before him, two formidable weapons, as he brought the full force of his violent emotions into focus upon Fedhisss, who stood there, fascinated, until the man started toward him.

Fedhisss lifted his camera. Hesitating for a fraction of a second, he wanted to savor the delightful moment. It was such an impressive experience, one that he had never known, never even dreamed of, seeing that murderous look gleaming with such a pitch of intensity out of the man's eyes.

But all good things had to end. "Say cheeeeese!" and he smiled to show the man how. Then he pressed the lever.

Fedhisss was about to leave when another student entered the laboratory.

"Whoa!" the student said, looking around at the mess. "I'll be damned if I'm going to clean it up. Where's Ed? I usually replace him about this time."

"He's taken off," Fedhisss said.

"Oh, oh," the student said. "Where's Bingo? Ed didn't take him out again, did he? The shit will really hit the fan."

"Bingo, I can say for sure," Fedhisss stifled a chuckle, "is mixing it up with Professor Jurgens."

"Ah," the student said. "The good professor. You a friend of his?"

"Yes," Fedhisss said.

"What's he up to now? I'm one of his lab assistants. You'd think I'd know. But I can hardly keep up with everything he's into."

"This time," Fedhisss said, and the chuckle slipped out, "he may have spread himself too thin. He asked you to wait for him here in the lab. And don't worry about the mess. He said he'd take care of it. But he did want you to do a favor for me."

"Sure." The student smiled to show his readiness to help.

"I'll be coming back here in a while," Fedhisss said. "I'll have an acquaintance with me, a very shy man who doesn't like to have his picture taken. When we walk into the lab, before he can say no, will you just take a quick picture of the two of us with this camera?"

"Hey, no problem," the student said taking the camera. "I haven't seen one like this before." He frowned as he turned it over in his hands.

"It's a new digital," Fedhisss said. "An experimental model.

I'm testing it for the manufacturer. Just sight the two of us through here, and when you have us framed, press this level on the side."

"You got it," the student said.

"And remember," Fedhisss said, "don't let him know in advance. Just raise the camera and click when we enter the lab."

"Camera shy, is he?" The student smiled.

"You'll see for yourself." Fedhisss returned the smile. "He goes to pieces."

30.

"HELLO, MAX. IS THIS a bad time?" Les had stopped in Professor Lichte's office doorway when he saw the professor, seated at his desk, concentrating on something he was writing.

Professor Lichte looked up, and his face brightened. "Dr. Marks, come in, come in." He stood with some effort, a small man of frail body, but with a shock of wild white hair, and vibrant gray eyes with an unsettling energy behind them. "My favorite literature teacher," he said. He caught sight then of Urr standing behind Les. "Ah, and I see you have brought back Mr. Feders with you. Come in, gentlemen."

Les exchanged a quick look with Urr as they entered the office. "He's been here," Les said to Urr.

"Evidently," Urr said. He looked around the office at the large desk, studiously cluttered, the bookcases carefully crammed with odd-sized books, the top of an old filing cabinet neatly piled too high with various printed materials about to spill over. Professor Lichte apparently tried to keep everything in its proper place, but the room still gave an impression of unattained order, of a level of harmony desired but not achieved within a small roomful of ever-present discordant forces.

A large chart of the periodic table was hanging on the wall behind the desk. Urr began to study it.

"Please sit, gentlemen," Professor Lichte said, gesturing to the two chairs facing his desk. "My old bones are finding it increasingly difficult to stay erect these days." When they had settled themselves, Professor Lichte looked expectantly at each of them.

"Max," Les said, struggling for a story to explain Urr's appearance, "this is Dr. Urr. He's actually Mr. Feders' twin brother. We've been looking for Mr. Feders around the campus. Can you tell me when he was here last?"

Professor Lichte smiled widely and waggled his finger at Les. "You wouldn't pull an old man's leg now, would you, Dr. Marks? His twin brother, you say." He considered Urr. "Separated, I assume, at birth. And only one of them is the rightful heir to the crown, which the other has maliciously stolen. A dastardly deed." He chuckled and waggled his finger again. "For someone who teaches the world's great works of literature, surely you can come up with something better than that."

"I'm serious, Max," Les said, looking somberly at him.

Professor Lichte was a little taken aback. "Good heavens, you are, aren't you!" He laughed aloud then and turned to Urr. "My apologies, Dr. Urr." He peered intensely now at Urr's face. "An amazing resemblance, even to the clothes you wear."

Urr nodded and shrugged a bit, as though he had heard the same remark too many times now. "On the surface we are indeed identical twins. But within, I can assure you, there are elemental differences."

"But why the different name, if I may ask?" Professor Lichte said.

"It's a professional one I assumed earlier to differentiate us," Urr said. "It helps with the confusion that always arises when we are together."

Professor Lichte appeared now unable to stop studying Urr. "What is your field, Dr. Urr? Please don't tell me that it is the same as your brother's."

It was Urr's turn to laugh. "And what did my brother tell you was his? He can be quite the jokester."

"Oh, he was most serious when we talked earlier this morning," Professor Lichte said, frowning now as he recalled the conversation. "He was quite excited about pursuing a rather difficult concept. The essentially neutral charge existing within a living cell. But apparently he wished to approach the subject from a technician's perspective, and so, I'm afraid, I was of little help to him. Do you share that interest with your brother?"

"Only indirectly," Urr said. "He is apparently focusing on the complex functioning of a single living cell. I'm more interested at the moment in the evolution of life here on earth, and particularly in the emergence of life out of inanimate matter."

"Oooh," Professor Lichte said, holding up his hands as though surrendering. "That will require you to make a great leap of faith, from physics into metaphysics."

"Not necessarily," Urr said. "I was thinking more along the lines of Schrodinger's classic little book *What Is Life?* Or Richard Feynman's work."

"Dr, Urr," Professor Lichte appealed with a kindly look, "this world already has too many reductionist physicists. Science and its rational approach to knowledge is only a part, and indeed a very small part, of this unfathomable universe. Here," he pulled open a side drawer in his desk and began rummaging through it. "I keep this here to remind me what a narrowminded idiot I can easily become." He pulled out a sheet of paper and began reading from it. "'There is nothing new in physics which needs to be discovered in order to understand the phenomena of life.'" He glanced up, smiling, and then continued reading. "'All ordinary phenomena can be explained by the actions and the motions of particles.'

Hah!" He waved the paper. "If only we knew what a particle is, then, perhaps, we could make such grand statements. Do you know who made these? It was Richard Feynman." Professor Lichte's eyes gleamed with amusement. "And here is my most favorite one, from Stephen Hawking, who made this claim just a few years ago. 'There are grounds for cautious optimism that we may now be near the end of the search for the ultimate laws of nature.' What an unfortunately inadequate phrase, 'the ultimate laws of nature,' when applied to a universe that is continuously evolving into something that has never existed before." He looked up then and shook his head slightly. "I simply cannot understand it. Why would the good Dr. Hawking say something like that?"

After waiting a moment as the professor mulled over his own question, Urr said, softly, "Perhaps because it arises out of a very human need."

"Oh?" said Professor Lichte. "A human need?" He refocused a penetrating gaze on Urr. "And what would that be?"

"To believe," Urr said, "that his presence within this world will not end with his death."

Judging from the professor's expression, Urr had obviously touched a tender spot, for the professor, too, within the deepest recesses of his mind, beneath the extensively accumulated facts and figures of his science, yearned to believe that his own intellectual accomplishments, recognized by so many of his peers, would give him a persisting presence, keep him somehow alive, within a world of indifferent forces that were soon to end his life.

Still looking closely at Urr, Professor Lichte nodded slowly. "Of course, you are right. I should be more understanding of Dr. Hawking's needs, as I would wish others to be more understanding of mine. I sit here, assuming that I have grounded my life upon a solid rock of reasoning, but what an ocean of ignorance surrounds me, a vast expanse in all directions out to my most distant horizons. And yet how often, and how easily, I live my life upon my little patch of ground, as though it were the entire world.

"Yes, I plead guilty to wanting my work to persist beyond me. And not simply through my writings, but within the minds of others. And not simply as a recollection, but as something more vibrant, something existing and evolving on its own within the minds of future lives. Is that possible?" he said, mostly to himself, not expecting a response. "As a physicist, I have a most difficult time with the old mind/body dichotomy. Does the mind somehow persist beyond the death of the body? That is a question that has rumbled like thunder down through the ages. Oh, what I would give to have the answer to it." The strength of the professor's desire to know, coming very close to pain, filled his eyes as he looked at each of them.

"Socrates," Urr said softly, "was called the wisest man in this world because he knew what he did not know."

Les looked at Urr, surprised by the comment. "Where did you pick that up?"

"Speaking of picking things up," Urr said, getting up from his chair and moving around the desk to stand beside Professor Lichte, "there's a bit of fuzz here caught in your hair."

As he reached out toward Professor Lichte's head, the professor scooted his chair back away from Urr. "Oh, no, not again! Not another spark! Your brother touched me earlier, the side of my head. Static electricity, he said. It almost knocked me down. What is it with you and your brother? Do you always go around zapping old men?"

Urr laughed and held up his hands to show that he had nothing in them. Then he reached out again. But Professor Lichte drew back further and, frowning now, looked at Urr warily. "Why do you want to touch my head?"

"Call it an experiment," Urr said. "In how many ways are my brother and I identical? Will my touch also create a spark of static electricity? If it does, will it be different? Weaker? Stronger? A lightning bolt! Or just a fizzle. Aren't you curious?"

It was the right approach, the appeal to curiosity, which Professor Lichte could never resist in whatever situation he found himself. As Urr reached slowly out again, the professor sat still this time and watched closely as Urr's finger came into contact with the side of his head. He jerked then, as though shocked, and grabbed the arms of his chair to steady himself. "The same," he said. "But different this time." He was clearly shaken. "The question I raised earlier," he said. "Consciousness...the mind/body...apparently I can see now that...." His eyes filled with wonder. "My God." He touched the side of his head, as though expecting to find something there. "How did you do that, Dr. Urr?"

"A simple exchange," Urr said. "A fair trade. And I thank you for all that you have given me."

Professor Lichte raised his eyebrows. "I've given you nothing to speak of."

"But you have," Urr said, as he came back around the desk and started for the door. "You've given me," his hand swept out, "everything." His gesture took in the entire office, the bookshelves and wall hangings, the cluttered desk, and the small, frail man seated at it.

Les stood up and started to follow him out. "Many thanks, Max. We want to catch Professor Jurgens before lunch. Dr. Urr will be interested in his thoughts on evolution, and what he's done with Bingo. I hope we didn't waste your time."

"Waste my time?" Professor Lichte said, still struggling mentally to reach solid ground again. "I believe that I have just been through a most unusual experience." He looked at Les, frowning, still clearly confused. "But I have absolutely no idea what it was that he did." He touched the side of his head again. "Can you tell me, Dr. Marks?"

Les paused in the doorway and looked back, smiling softly. "It would take too great a leap of faith."

"From physics into metaphysics?"

"No." Les considered. "From physics to...." He hesitated.

"To what?" Professor Lichte urged.

Les nodded slowly, as though recognizing the truth of it. "Reality," he said.

31.

"IT'S DOWN AT THE end of this hall," Les said to Urr, as they made their way through the building toward the biology laboratory. "Professor Jurgens is a noted authority on evolution, with a speciality in language development. The work he's done with Bingo is really remarkable. About three hundred words, I think. Many of his colleagues didn't believe he could do it."

"Is this the proverbial simian," Urr said, "that randomly hits typewriter keys until a Shakespearean play appears?"

Les glanced at him, smiling. "Where are you picking up such things?"

Classes were in session, so the halls were almost empty, but a coed coming out of one of the offices called to Les. "Professor Marks? Professor? Could I ask you something, please?" She hurried toward him.

Les stopped, letting Urr walk on. "Yes, Mary, what is it?"

She was a rather large young woman, with unkempt hair and a nose ring. Les knew and liked her as someone with a deep emotional attachment to the best literature she was studying. "In class this morning," she said, "you were referring to a good article on *Moby-Dick.* I should have written it down, and now I've forgotten."

"No problem, Mary. It's one of my favorites, in the summer 1969 issue of *Sewanee Review.*"

"Thank you, Professor. I'm off to the library. I'll look it up."

She smiled and waved as she started away, already looking forward, he could tell, to finding the article. The perfect student, he thought, and he relished the feeling as it moved through him. What a pleasure to teach.

Urr was nearing the biology laboratory when a student started out of its door and saw him. "Whoa!" the student said, his face brightening with recognition. He went quickly back into the lab.

When Les caught up, he saw Urr frowning and looking into the lab through the glass paneling in the door. "What is it?" he said. "Nobody there?"

"Yes," Urr said. "A student. But he's acting somewhat peculiar."

Les smiled. "Don't let it surprise you. They all do, at one time or another." He held the door open for Urr and followed him into the lab.

"Hold it right there!" the student said, bringing up a device before his face. "Smile for the birdie!" He centered the two of them in the frame of the device and put his finger on the level at the side. Then he looked up over the contraption. "Professor Marks? It's you? The one who's so camera shy? I never would have guessed it." He looked through the device again, centering them in the frame. "Honestly, it won't hurt a bit—"

"No!" Urr said, and lunged forward, knocking the weapon up just as the student pressed the lever down. The device had been clicked as it was pointing upward toward a portion of the ceiling, catching within its frame a housefly that had landed up there.

A *phfft* was heard.

Urr glanced up as a small cloud appeared and began to drift along the ceiling.

"Hey!" the student said, looking upset. "If you didn't want me to, why did you ask?"

"I'm sorry," Urr said. "That was rude of me. But I changed my mind since I was here. I didn't want to impose on Dr. Marks."

The student, with some effort, shrugged it off. "Well, it's your camera." He handed the device to Urr, who examined it and then, appearing to lose his grip, let it drop to the floor, where it broke open into pieces.

"Or at least it was," the student said, bending down to pick up the pieces. "Doesn't look like it's good for much now."

Urr reached out and selected one small part from the student's hand. "Keep the rest," Urr said. "Someone might still find some use for the parts. But I'm sorry to lose that great picture you took of the ceiling."

"Yeah," the student said, smiling now. "Action shot."

Urr appeared to be trying to recall something. "I can't remember. Was I carrying anything else when I was here last?"

"Just that larger metal box," the student said.

Urr nodded while slipping the part he had taken into a small slot on the back of his belt.

"You must be one of Professor Jurgens' lab assistants," Les said. "Is he in the area?" Les looked around. "I don't see Bingo, either."

The student was looking at Urr, puzzled. "I thought you knew where he was."

"No," said Urr. "I lost track of him."

"Well," the student said, "he can't be going too far if he's got Bingo with him. The cage is still empty." He walked over and looked in through the bars. "But with one hell of a mess in there. Damn! Who's going to clean that up?" He gestured around the immediate area. "And all this other sticky stuff. And look here. Somebody's been taking their clothes off and just dumping them there and there on the floor. Who would do something like that in here?" It was clearly troubling him. He turned back to them. "The professor would never, not for even a second, put up with a mess like that."

Urr walked over to the cage and looked in.

"What do you think it is?" the student said.

"I believe," said Urr, with a thoughtful look, "it's Bingo."

"You mean Bingo made that mess?" the student said.

"No," said Urr. "I mean Bingo *is* that mess."

"Christ!" said Les, looking distraught. "And the two piles of clothes? You mean Fedhisss—"

"Yes," said Urr, turning back to Les. "He did give me a fair warning, and apparently he's ready now."

"To do what?" Les said, his voice rising.

The student was looking back and forth at them, trying to make sense of what they were saying.

"Why, to shatter me, of course. And everyone around me."

Les stared at Urr, transfixed, struggling to take it in. "You've got to do something! You can't let him do that!"

As though he had just thought of something more important, Urr focused a questioning look on Les.

"How does that make you feel?"

32.

Les came out of the office marked *Director, Science and Technology Center*. Urr was waiting for him in the hall. "I spoke with his secretary. He's gone to the cafeteria for lunch. Do we have the time to go looking for him? What's the point, Urr? Why do you want to see him?"

Urr appeared somewhat distracted. "Tell me, Les. How do human beings gain their greatest truths? By thinking clearly, or by feeling deeply?"

Les was obviously edgy now. "What has that got to do with our stopping Fedhisss?"

"His present containment, to some degree, will influence the way he functions."

"You mean, he'll think more like a human being?"

"And particularly feel more."

"What difference will that make, Urr? He's killing people! Whatever causes him to act now, we've got to stop him!"

"It could play a role in our doing so. Perhaps a decisive one."

Les looked perplexed. "What does all this have to do with the Director of this Center?"

"You have told me, have you not, that the Director is one of your best scientists."

"Absolutely. Professor Enders has published in most of the leading scientific journals. He's an impressive generalist, a coordinator of the different branches of science, with an appropriate background for that task. That's why he was made Director."

"Would you consider him to be capable of thinking objectively, unencumbered by his own emotions?"

Les spoke as though stating the obvious. "He's a man of science, for God's sake."

Urr nodded seriously at the mixed expression. "Then, for God's sake, let's go find him, this highly educated and accomplished man of science. It may help me to understand better what is happening within Fedhisss, causing his thoughts to be diverted in such oddly irrational ways. At what point, Les, does any rational being step across the line into irrationality?"

"You want to ask Professor Enders that question?"

"No, Les. I want to see him doing so."

"Become irrational?" Les considered the possibility, and then shook his head. "I think you're going to be disappointed, Urr."

"Perhaps," Urr said. "Shall we go and see?"

As they entered the cafeteria, there was a general hum of conversation filling the room, mixed with the sounds of silverware and plates being used. Les glanced around until he spotted the professor off to the left. "There he is," he said to Urr, and led the way as they weaved through the tables, occupied mostly by students.

Professor Enders looked up from his tray as they approached. He was a short and plumpish man, middle-aged, with a rounded face and features that bespoke a nature generally willing to be agreeable. His thinning brown hair was combed slightly forward to hide his receding hairline. "Dr. Marks," he said, smiling, "and my morning visitor. Welcome again," he said to Urr. "I'm sorry I had to rush off and leave you that way. Did you get to see enough of the Center?"

"Yes, thank you," Urr said, ignoring Les's troubled look. "Very impressive. You must be pleased to be the Director."

"Oh, it has its good moments. But it also keeps me awfully tied up, one meeting after another. I have little time to pursue my own interests." He looked from Urr to Les. "If you two are here for lunch, why don't you join me? I'm sorry, but I never got my morning visitor's name." He looked expectantly at Urr.

"This is Dr. Urr," Les said. "He's here just for the day." They nodded pleasantly at each other. "We'd like very much to join you." He turned to Urr. "I'll show you the way through the line."

Les led Urr to an area stacked with trays and containers of silverware. They took what they needed and made their way around a wall to enter the line, pushing their trays along the rack in front of the staff serving the food. "Let's see," Les said. "What can we eat quickly? Pork chops. A vegetarian lasagna. And the ever-present hotdogs and hamburgers."

Urr looked at each of the containers of food, his face settling into a frown of concern. "I believe that I would be least troubled if I continued ingesting the lower life forms, like the pie I had yesterday and the toast you gave me this morning."

"Then we'll both take the vegetarian lasagna," Les said, signaling to the woman serving. "And some string beans on the side." They made their way along the line. "And a carton of milk." He put one on Urr's tray. "And some chocolate cake for dessert." He considered what they had taken. "Nothing there will bite you back, Urr."

Urr looked somewhat dubiously at the food on his tray.

As they returned to the table, Les was surprised to see Anne sitting there with her tray of food.

Professor Enders beamed at her. "Look who I've also managed to lure to my table. It must be my lucky day."

"Oh, Les," she said when she saw him, clearly troubled. "I'm sorry, I didn't realize. I won't intrude." She started to rise.

"Nonsense!" Professor Enders said. "I'm sure that Dr. Marks would be delighted to have you join us." He smiled

questioningly at Les, with a hint of amusement at Les's reaction. It was general knowledge around the campus that
the two of them had been seeing each other.

"Of course," Les said, trying to be casual. Anne looked at
him closely, trying to read his response. He held her look a
moment, feeling good things moving within him behind his
confusion. "Please stay," he appealed to her.

She smiled shyly and sat again. Les and Urr took the remaining seats, and they all settled themselves comfortably
and began to eat from their trays.

"Dr. Urr," Professor Enders said, "what brings you to
our campus?"

Urr considered the question a moment and then answered. "I'm researching a report that I'm writing on the
emergence and evolution of life on this planet."

"Really?" The subject obviously interested the professor.
"There have been a good many books on that subject."

"But not written from the viewpoint I am taking."

"Which is?" Professor Enders said.

"That of an extraterrestrial alien."

Les started coughing as he choked on his food.

The professor glanced at Les and then, frowning, back to
Urr. "Why an alien? Is it a science-fiction book?"

"No," Urr said. "A serious study."

"Then I repeat my question. Why an alien?"

"Greater objectivity," Urr said. "Outside of the whimsical-
ities of human nature. I am an alien on a long journey with
a very specific purpose."

The professor raised his eyebrows, waiting for an explanation.

Urr continued to look expressionless at him. "To seek out
and categorize other forms of life existing within the universe."

"Ah," the professor said. "Now there is a subject worthy of
attention. Are there, indeed, other forms of life within the uni-

verse, or are we simply some erratic squiggle that has emerged against unbelievable odds, to be carried along within a universe expanding ever outward, until it finally...well...there's the question. Until it finally does...what?" He was looking at Urr, but his eyes were dimmed, his thoughts having wandered somewhere out to the edge of his own imagined universe.

Mentally exceeding the speed of light, Professor Enders returned to earth and smiled at Urr. "I must welcome you, then, to our planet. I hope you are having a pleasant and productive visit." He was clearly amused by the conversation, and willing to play along.

Anne was watching Urr with a more serious expression.

33.

URR ATE A BIT more of his food, and then put his fork down beside his plate. He studied Professor Enders a moment. "I'll be making out my report soon. Would you like to hear what I am going to say?"

"I would, indeed," Professor Enders said, pleased to have a diverting break from the duties awaiting him back in his office. "Fire away."

"Obviously, I will have some difficulty in conveying my findings within the limits of a human language."

"Of course," Professor Enders said. "That's an old problem faced by most aliens. How can you convey your concepts to us when we have no words to express them? But give it your best try."

"And since," Urr said, "we do not have much time—"

"That's right!" Les said intensely beneath his breath.

Urr nodded and then paused a moment as he looked carefully at each person around the table. "When I first arrived here, my primary concern quickly became that of wanting to know how it was possible that life forms around this planet were destroying other life forms. Even human beings, the most advanced form, have been killing each other throughout their history, as though it were a necessary part of their existence. I wanted to know if that was true."

Professor Enders sat back in his chair, the look of amusement replaced now by a slight frown as he watched Urr.

"Tell me, Professor Enders," Urr said. "What was the first time, in the evolution of life on this planet, that one creature killed another? In other words, what was the first form of life to become murderous? And I would also like to know if human beings have descended from that form."

"Let me think a moment," Professor Enders said, brushing a few strands of hair off his forehead, as though clearing the ground for action. "Humankind as a life form emerged about three million years ago, or four million, or five million," he waggled his hand, "depending upon which paleontologist you read, already possessing the capacity to kill. Before that point were primates, back to about sixty million years ago. Then the first appearance of mammals about three hundred million years ago. Then reptiles, including dinosaurs. Then amphibians, then the higher fishes, then the first vertebrates about six hundred to seven hundred million years ago, again depending upon which paleontologist you are reading."

"Did they all kill?" Urr asked.

"Yes," the professor nodded, "voraciously." He paused again to gather his thoughts. "Then the first multicellular invertebrates, about seven hundred million years ago. Then single nucleated cells, back to about 1.4 billion years ago."

"They also killed?"

"Yes. Then single cells with no nuclei, better known as bacteria, that stayed around in that state back to about three and a half billion years ago, back to the first appearance of life on earth."

"They—"

"Yes," Professor Enders said, and he shrugged slightly. "The course of nature."

"It sounds more like the ultimate murder mystery," Urr said. "Everyone is guilty. Next, I would like to know what the energy output of your sun is."

"Well," the professor smiled, "it's not *my* sun, but, offhand, I couldn't give you an exact figure."

"Would it be correct to say that, within the sun, four tons of hydrogen are being transformed every second into heat and sunlight, and that Earth receives some minuscule fraction of that energy?"

Professor Enders laughed. "That sounds about right." He turned to Anne and Les. "Just imagine that. Every second. Four *tons* of hydrogen turned into energy. Amazing, isn't it?"

"Do you really believe so?" Urr asked, looking somewhat dubious. "I would have characterized it as a rather mediocre energy output, if compared to any spectrum of stars."

"Technically true," the professor said, "but it's the only sun we have, so I tend to admire it, since we're all so obviously dependent upon it as we float around it on our little blue dot."

"Exactly," Urr said. "It's the only sun you have. And it unlocks the answer to the question I raised earlier. Why all the killing upon this planet?" He paused, looking at each of them. "It's an interesting question, with a terrible answer, for what I eventually discovered was this," he said. "And I will convey it," he turned again to Professor Enders, "in your own language."

Les and Anne sat quietly, listening closely to their conversation.

As Urr continued, he watched Professor Enders. "Each and every member of the multitude of life forms presently existing here on earth, including each of you, is a transitory part of an unbroken line that can be traced back down through the many branchings of preexisting physical forms, down through the first appearance of the most rudimentary life forms, until we reach that flickering and fragile moment when two insignificant bits of matter, two different and physically separated atoms, were first nudged together and into a direction they had never taken before on this once inanimate planet. And then what happened? Mystery of mysteries! They began to reproduce themselves. And they have been at it, unceasingly, ever since." He leaned forward, frowning seriously. "At this point in your history, whatever anyone believes or claims, nobody really knows how that initial act occurred."

Where was he going with this? Les thought.

Urr put his elbows on the table and folded his hands in front of his face, watching Professor Enders over the tops of his knuckles. "You scientists have, to your credit, made some progress. You've managed to uncover a few new facts about life's emergence into physical forms. But unfortunately they proved to be uncomfortable facts, with implications that caused you to shy away and do your best to ignore them."

It was Professor Enders' turn to look dubious. "Such as?"

"Such as," Urr said. "Listen carefully. Life on this planet exists because of a rudimentary process that uses the energy emitted by your sun to construct physical containments for various levels of consciousness. That energy conversion was necessary for those atoms I mentioned earlier to begin accumulating into molecules, and the molecules into one-celled creatures, and the one-celled into multi-celled creatures. But along that very early pathway, something terrible happened. The energy conversion rate proved to be inadequate to support the larger, more active life forms that evolved from this process. Life, in its early emergence, began to learn through trial and error that it had to play by the rules of the mechanistic universe. One such rule was that more advanced physical forms could not be constructed and maintained here without greater amounts of readily available organic energy. Sunlight or inorganic chemical sources cannot fulfill that need here on earth, unless over time they are gathered and condensed into more intensified energy packets. But such a gathering of energy was available only within one source. The physical forms of life that had already been created. The larger and more active forms could not have emerged and evolved, and this is the remarkable point, except by ingesting the accumulated energy to be found within, and being utilized by, other life forms."

He frowned again and dropped his gaze to the desktop, resting his forehead on his folded hands, as though he were praying. He was clearly troubled by his own thoughts. "I cannot conceive of a more deplorable elementary energy system for supporting the emergence and development of life, based as it is on the suffering and the death of so many varieties of consciousness to be found around this entire planet."

Then he looked, unseeing, off to one side and, after musing for a long moment, brought forth a final thought. "If I were trying to conceive of a god to worship, the last thing I would ever think of assigning to that deity is the creation of life on this world."

They sat there, unmoving, as Urr's last remark sank in.

"What I am offering you," Urr said softly, "is another perspective of what exists here, an alien perspective. Consider for a moment the alien writing my report. As part of his journey, he has been assigned the responsibility of deciding if the life forms he encounters on his travels are of a nature worthy enough to justify their continued existence within his universe. What will he decide, what judgment will he reach, concerning all of the life forms inhabiting this particular planet?" Urr turned for a moment to Les and Anne with a sympathetic look, as though he regretted having to tell them. "What other possible judgment could the alien reach? He will deem the destructive life forms created here to be unworthy of existence."

Sadly, he shook his head. "Including each of you."

34.

No one spoke then, as they struggled uncomfortably with the perspective they had just been offered, a general condemnation of the nature of all life on Earth.

Across the room, a table of students broke out into laughter. They rose noisily as a group, pushing back their chairs with loud scrapings and heading toward the exit.

Urr watched them depart, and then looked again at Professor Enders, who finally appeared to break free. "Wait, now! Just one moment! Aren't you being too heavy-handed? There are other conclusions that could just as well be reached from your comments."

"Such as?" Urr said.

"Such as," Professor Enders said, leaning forward, his elbows on the table. "Try this on for size." He looked up for a moment, as though searching for some higher thought. Then he focused again on Urr. "During a particular period of time in the evolution of the universe, life arose spontaneously on earth because of a unique conjunction of materials and forces. It could not have happened otherwise, as we have established scientifically beyond any doubt within a variety of related fields." His voice then took on an edge. "And so it is not open to moralizing criticisms. Whatever its shortcomings, it is the best there is, and we had better damned well take it as it is, and be pleased that we have been fortunate enough to have emerged at the top of the food chain supporting it. Emerged, I might add, as a distinctive species, with the most advanced intelligence." The professor sat back then and visibly relaxed, looking somewhat amused at Urr for having presumed to challenge him.

"Tell me, Professor," Urr said softly. "Do you believe that a human being possesses the traditional five senses of touch, sight, hearing, smell, and taste?"

The professor considered, somewhat wary of making any quick answers. "Ruling out the unsubstantiated claims to extra-sensory perception, yes, I believe that, as a human being, I possess those five senses."

"But I would argue," Urr said, "that you possess only one sense. Seeing, hearing, smelling, tasting are all forms of touch. As you peer through the telescope, you believe that you *see* the planets, stars, distant galaxies, the universe in all its depth and perspective, only because photons of light make contact with your eyes, and your brain interprets the contact. Your experience of the entire material universe is limited to the surface of your body. Life here on Earth, in other words, is still feeling its way into the universe."

The professor swept out with his hand, as though brushing aside Urr's remarks. "The telescope, the spectroscope, the electron microscope. Scientific instrumentation, increasingly across the ages, has *dramatically* extended our capacities to perceive. The direction of your argument is simply a fallacious one. Just look at the impressive and *consistent* body of scientific knowledge that we have gathered about this universe."

"Consistent," Urr said, nodding, as though agreeing. "Yes, I can see what you mean. From the early astronomical and mathematical conclusions reached by Ptolemy and others, to the belief that a homunculus, a little human being, could be found within the sperm of a male, that plagues were caused by planetary corruptions of the atmosphere, that maggots could generate spontaneously out of garbage, that the atom was undoubtedly the smallest building-block of matter, that space and time were fixed and unrelated concepts, that the major land masses of the Earth have always been in their present positions, that the age of the universe is five billion years, or is it fifty billion years, or ten or fifteen billion years. Yes, there has definitely been a consistency in your scientific knowledge."

As Urr had gone on through the list, Professor Ender's face had become increasingly flushed, as though a head of steam were building up inside him. "I'm not referring to old and outmoded beliefs." He glared at Urr. "I am referring to the consistency in the findings that have recently been achieved throughout the sciences. Would you deny that?"

"I would deny that consistency, by itself, is any kind of objective accomplishment. Ptolemy's system of a geocentric universe was wonderfully consistent in its day. Out of the multitude of stars throughout the heavens, there were only a small handful of wanderers. But they led to the conception of an entirely different universe."

"And you think that's where we are today?" He offered Urr an exaggerated look of astonishment. "A consistent set of erroneous beliefs?"

Urr considered. "I would not call them erroneous."

"Well," the professor said, drawing out the word, "that's awfully big of you."

"No," Urr said, "not erroneous. I would call them currently accepted fictions that meet your need to think you know. It allows you to cover over your deeper and more uncomfortable awareness that you simply don't know." Urr smiled softly as he watched the professor.

"What nonsense!" Professor Enders blurted out. "What balderdash!" It was an old expression that he particularly liked, one that he felt always confounded his opponents. He raised his right hand, about to propound an objection, and pointed his index finger at Urr, as though he were going to skewer him with it.

"Professor Enders! Professor!" A woman had entered the cafeteria and was calling across to them.

"It's your secretary," Les said.

"Your one-thirty! They're waiting for you!"

"Damn!" Professor Enders said, glancing at his watch. "I've got to run." He stood up quickly, but then paused a moment, looking down at Urr. "Well," he said, and he was the Director again, slipping comfortably into his role as he would a favorite jacket. "Although I did find your ideas a bit too spacey, Dr, Urr"—he paused, smiling, to let the pun sink in—"it was certainly a diverting conversation." He turned to Les. "Where did you find this interesting man, Dr. Marks?"

Les shrugged. "He just dropped out of the blue."

"Of course!" Professor Enders said. "How else would an alien arrive?" He waved goodbye, and hurried across the room, quickly dismissing the three of them from his mind as he headed for his next meeting.

Anne continued watching Urr closely, with a deeply puzzled look. What was there about this man, his unassuming and calm presence, that left her feeling so disquieted? Like one of the wandering stars moving inauspiciously across Ptolemy's sky, he gave her the sense that something ominously discomforting about her world was in the wind, and it was blowing her way now.

35.

THEY SAT THERE QUIETLY.

"It's all a bit too much for me," Les said. "I'll have to live with it awhile to see what I think."

"And you, Miss Sommers?" Urr said.

She shook her head slightly, for another thought had just occurred to her. "If I assume that everything you said is true, it still does not account for one of our worst characteristics."

Urr waited for her to continue.

"Perhaps the very worst, as I think about it. It's the question you raised earlier, which you haven't really answered yet. Why are human beings so unnecessarily destructive? I can understand life forms killing other life forms for the food they need to survive. Human beings obviously need to do that. But what about all the other acts of cruelty and death that we inflict so often upon each other? How do you explain that part of our nature?"

"Yes," Urr said, his face darkening into a frown. "What explains that?" He studied Anne a moment. "I will offer you another uncomfortable thought. The degree of all human suffering in this world can be measured by the depth of human ignorance."

She considered his answer. "But if we are aware of our essential ignorance?"

"If only each of you was truly aware," Urr said. "What a difference that would make in all human interactions."

"But why do you think we're not?" she said.

"Because across your history, human beings have always avoided facing the depths of their ignorance. And they have done so primarily by convincing themselves that, through their religions or their sciences, they have already achieved, or are about to achieve, ultimate knowledge of the universe and their place within it." He shook his head sadly. "Human beings are cruel to each other because they assume that they know what they are doing."

"Are we stuck at that level?" Les said, leaning forward.

Urr smiled and brightened a bit. "Life here on Earth still recognizes the need to continue feeling its way into the universe. And that, perhaps, is the encouraging point. As a species awakened involuntarily upon this planet, you found yourselves caught within the dire circumstances of a deplorable energy system. That you have managed to survive and to evolve to this point is a remarkable accomplishment."

"But where do we go from here?" Les said.

"That's the part that interests me most," Urr said. "Your having reached this level of consciousness is an unexpected emergence out of the conditions that have brought forth life on this planet. But for too long now that consciousness has been threatened by an underlying fear of the uncontrolled forces shaping its existence. It has caused you, persistently across your history, to inflict upon each other senseless acts of destruction and death. And yet I have also discovered, much to my surprise, that even during the unfolding of those deplorable circumstances, another unexpected emergence has been taking place within your species." He smiled softly at both of them. "I find it most interestingly, though somewhat erratically, illustrated by you two."

Les and Anne glanced at each other. "Which is?" Les said to Urr.

"Something more than the physical interactions of your species," Urr said. "Something other than your material nature, which is still functioning according to the rules of the mechanistic universe. What I am referring to is still too intertwined with your physical nature, but it is beginning, just beginning, to transcend it. If it does indeed continue emerging as one of your more distinctive characteristics, it will play a decisive role in easing the persisting cruelties of human existence."

He saw them both frowning, still waiting for some clarification of what he was referring to.

"Within the more recent history of your species," he said, "the word that is generally used to describe it is love."

Glancing again at Anne, Les felt the old confusion arising within him. She had colored a bit, but her face was filled with a radiance that revealed her feelings. "I don't understand," Les said to Urr. "I'm...."

"Yes," Urr said, "I know. But you are much closer to each other than you realize." He looked carefully at each of them. "Perhaps I could be of some help here by letting you see for yourself, Les." He held up both hands to show that they were empty, and then reached out to touch Les on the side of his head.

"Oh, no," Les said, looking plaintively at Urr. "Not again."

36.

ALONG THE DIRT ROAD, *after school, the four of them walked home together. Jim and Phil stayed close to Shelley.*

Anne lagged behind.

"Chuk-a-choo!" Phil yelled, running and jumping straight up from the road. Grabbing the seat of his pants, "Ree-booo!" he pulled up as he jumped again. He came back, bright-eyed, to tell them. "Just about!" His body would soon be flying.

Anne closed her eyes, shutting out the afternoon sunlight, and heard Jim. "Like a gooney bird." Laughing. Then Shelley said, "Did you ever hold a bird in your hand?"

Anne walked along into the darkness before her, only her feet touching the world, each step hoping to find the earth. The dirt road was in her mind now. "Uh!"

Her eyes popped open, and she saw them laughing. Phil had sneaked up and poked her in the stomach with his finger.

"What were you doing, Anne?" Shelley said.

"Trying to be like Ma!" Jim said.

Holding her stomach, Anne trailed again behind them, moving along the edge of the woods now.

"Your ma's not blind again, is she?" Phil widened his eyes, staring, and waved his hand back and forth in front of them.

"Ma was never blind," Jim said. "She just couldn't see."

"What's the difference?" Phil said.

Jim looked at Shelley. "Boy! What a gooney bird!" They laughed together. "The difference is..." he frowned now, "it was just for three days. Like closing your eyes that long. When you're blind, you don't ever see."

"Oh," Phil said. It kept them quiet a moment.

"I saw a blind man once," Shelley said. "His eyes looked all milky."

"Did you poke him one?" Phil said.

"I stayed away," Shelley said.

"Girls!" Phil said. "Fraidy-cats!"

"Girls can do anything a gooney can do," Jim said.

"They can't fly!" Phil said, running to the side of the road. "See this tree? See that branch sticking out? I could climb up there and sit on that if I wanted to."

"So could Shelley. Easy."

"She could not!"

Jim took Shelley's hand and led her to the tree. "Come on, Shelley. Show the gooney."

Anne watched from the road, wondering if Shelley was big enough yet for the tree.

Shelley looked up at the branch sticking out, then went to the tree and put her arms around it. Lifting her feet from the ground, she wrapped her bare legs around the trunk and began to inch her way upwards, her body tight against the tree.

She soon had made it almost half way up to the branch.

"You see, Phil?" Jim said. "What did I tell you?"

Puffing out his cheeks, Phil blew at her until his face turned red.

Anne, still watching her from the road, began to feel something happening now as Shelley further inched her body up the trunk, when suddenly, just before she reached the branch, Shelley started sliding quickly downwards. Anne held her breath as Shelley, near the ground again, clutched the tree once more, and shuddered, her eyes for the moment brightly frightened by the feeling. A point of almost pain flickered into Anne.

Jim and Phil waited uneasily by the tree, staring at Shelley as she stood up again, slightly bent, holding her body stiffly together.

Jim went closer to her. "You all right, Shelley?"

"I want to go home." She walked away from the tree, trying not to look at any of their eyes, and started up the road again.

They all lagged behind her now, separated from each other. Anne tried to walk closer to Jim, but he kept moving away, his eyes still on Shelley. Phil, trailing along the edge of the road, tried to watch a thin cloud passing overhead.

They walked apart from each other until they finally came to Phil's house, next door to Anne and Jim's.

"Hey, I know what!" Phil said. "I'll go in and ask my ma if we can lay on my grandma's feather bed."

Shelley kept walking.

"You want to try, Jim?" Phil said.

Jim turned from the road then. "All right."

"Anne, you coming?" Phil said.

"I'm going home," Anne said.

"Tell Ma where I am," Jim said. He went with Phil around toward the back door of Phil's house.

The feeling from the tree was still with Anne. She took a last look, in the late afternoon sunlight, at Shelley walking away from her down the dirt road. Then she went through her yard and around to the kitchen, opening the door. She wanted to ask her mother what had happened to Shelley.

"Momma, I'm home!"

A pot was simmering on the back of the stove.

At the sink she found a glass in the dish drainer and turned on the faucet, letting the water run until it was cold on her finger.

"Jim's staying over at Phil's house, Momma!"

Filling the glass, she drank slowly, wanting to feel the first cold swallows going down inside her. She left the empty glass by the drain.

"Momma?"

She stood by the sink and waited for an answer, listening now to the stillness in the house.

Going through the hallway, she looked into the frontroom. The couch and the armchairs were empty, the lamps unlit in the corners. All the furniture in the dim room seemed to be waiting for someone. Only the curtains by an open window moved with a breath of air.

She went back through the hallway to her mother's bedroom. The bed was neatly made. Draped across a chair were the clothes her mother had been wearing that morning.

Once more in the hallway, Anne stopped before the bathroom door, which was only slightly open.

"Momma?"

She put her hand on the door and pushed, and as the door swung open, she started in.

In front of her, on the floor of the shower, she saw her mother, crumpled.

Her breath, her heart, stopped for a moment. She was unable to move. Wide-eyed with a clutching fear, she struggled until she finally broke free and ran.

Through the kitchen and out the door, across the yard to Phil's house. She pressed herself against the side of the house, pounding with her fist on the wall. When no one came, she squatted down beside the house and cried.

A car came up the road and turned into the yard. Before it had stopped, Anne was running again. "Gramp! Gramp!"

Her grandfather turned off the engine and climbed out.

"Well, now! What have we here? Have you—" He saw her face and bent over, frowning. "What's wrong, Anne?"

"Momma!" she cried. "Something's happened to Momma!"

"Where, Anne? Where is she?"

"In the shower, Gramp. She's on the floor!"

Hurrying after him, Anne saw Jim come out of Phil's and run across the yard.

"Wait here," Gramp said to her in the kitchen. Jim came in. "Hey, what's the matter? Where's Gramp?"

"Something's happened to Momma, Jim."

Gramp came through the hallway, carrying her mother to the bedroom.

Jim stared, frightened, and then burst out crying. "Ma!"

Gramp carried her to the bed and pulled the bedspread over her body. Then he sat in the chair by the telephone and called the doctor and Anne's father. As he was making the calls, Anne and Jim, both still crying, came into the room. He let them have their look.

Staying close to Jim, Anne went near the bed and saw her mother lying stiffly under the covering, her eyes closed towards them, something soft having gone out of her face, leaving only rigid flesh.

They backed away, going into the kitchen again. Jim sat by the kitchen table, waiting for his father to come. Anne went outside and sat on the step to watch for his car.

When Gramp had finished with his calls and talked some to Jim in the kitchen, he came out and bent down next to Anne. The daylight was almost gone now, the darkness coming out of the woods.

"You're the woman of the family now, Anne. You remember that, will you?" He looked at her a moment and then went back inside.

Anne sat there on the step, trying to remember that she was the woman of the family, until she thought of wanting to ask her mother about the tree. In the gathering night it started her crying again, the feeling that she was alone now with the question.

37.

THE CAFETERIA HAD ALMOST emptied out. The few remaining students, talking softly, were emptying their trays and heading for the exit.

"Oh, Anne." The pained look on his face confused her. She clutched inside, holding herself together as the force of his feelings washed over her.

"What?" she said. "What is it, Les?"

"I'm so very sorry. It must have hurt you so much." His sense of her loss was moving inside him, a small maelstrom of swirling feelings that were stirring up and mixing together with his own childhood loss, intensifying the anguish he knew that she had experienced, so beyond the capacities of a small child to understand.

"I don't understand, Les," she said, pleading with him. "What's the matter?"

"I lost my own mother as a child," he said, the words rising up, seeking release, after being held inside for so long. "One day she was there, and then she wasn't."

A frightened look came into Anne's eyes. "I never told you. How do you know?" She felt a palpable threat to the sanity of her everyday world, the same threat she had experienced earlier with Urr in the small office in the library. "Please," she said. "Les. Please. Tell me what's going on here."

"I've been acting like such a fool," Les said. "As though I was the only one in the whole world who had been deeply hurt as a child. I've kept myself closed off for so many years, Anne, afraid of being hurt again. And then I met you. And it all became so confusing."

"But I've never told you," she persisted. "How do you know now?"

His face full of sorrow, he shrugged slightly and glanced at Urr, as though expecting him to explain. She saw the look and also turned to Urr, but he continued sitting quietly, calmly watching each of them. His bland features, still vaguely familiar to her, had an added sense now of something unknown, something mysterious, there behind his expressionless face. The perfect mask, she thought. The ubiquitous look of everyman.

"Who are you, really?" Anne said.

He offered her a pleasant look. "Someone who is trying to help you."

"Help me?" She frowned. "To do what?"

"To survive," he said.

"Survive what?" Her frown deepened.

Urr considered the question a moment. "My visit?" he answered, with a rueful smile.

The answer appeared to jar Les out of the emotional state he was caught in. "The time!" he said, looking at his watch, and then frantically at Urr.

"Yes," Urr said. "We must leave."

When she saw them both rise, she stood herself. "Please," she said to Urr, grasping after a last straw of explanation.

"Yes?" Urr paused, his eyebrows raised.

"When you were talking with us earlier, you kept referring to *us*"—she gestured to Les and herself—"as a species existing here on earth." She could sense within herself that this man was once again bringing her dangerously close to the edge of her known world. "But you didn't include yourself," she said, "as though you somehow didn't belong here. Why?" It was a simple question, but she believed that it held the key to everything.

She waited to see if he would answer.

38.

As THEY LEFT THE campus and turned onto the highway, heading back toward town, Les glanced at Urr, who was sitting calmly beside him, staring impassively ahead, as though he were seeing nothing beyond the limits of the windshield.

"Miss Sommers was not very happy when we left," Urr said.

"What did you expect?" Les said. "I keep telling her I'll explain later." He made a low, disparaging noise. "If I'm around later to explain."

"Do you believe she will stay there on the campus, as you have asked?"

"God, I hope so. I don't want to see her hurt." The thought made him press down more on the gas pedal, sending the car speeding along the road, well above the posted limit. He had to slow down only once, when they approached the area where the truck had been badly damaged by the tornado. Two police cars were parked beside the highway, their warning lights blinking. An officer motioned them to proceed slowly past the truck, lying on its side, still partway on the road, as a large crane and a highway crew prepared to move it. Les looked for the other cars that had been damaged, but apparently they had already been towed away, and he was able to resume his speed.

He glanced at Urr. "How can you be so sure that he's left the university?"

"I'm not," Urr said. "But we do know that he's carrying

a metallic case now, and I'm assuming that he has decided to use it first against your town. A trial run, perhaps. An initial test."

Les grimaced at the thought. "I don't see how you can stay so...untroubled," he said, groping for the word. "We couldn't find him on the campus. How do you expect to find him in town? There's so little time left."

"The metallic case that he is carrying, Les, judging from the device that I saw back in the laboratory, is something that he has designed to place a negative charge on the individual cells of a body. Opposite charges attract. Like charges repel. Apparently, his device succeeds. You saw the results there in the lab."

"Bingo, you mean?" Les's voice began to rise. "And the two piles of clothes? My God, Urr, we've got to stop him before he murders any more people."

"Not just people," Urr said.

"Are you telling me the metallic case is a larger version of that small device?"

Yes," Urr said. "He intends to shatter me, with a shotgun approach, you might say. A single blast upon the town, when he thinks that I am there. And since he knows that I am following him, it could be any time now. But I do not believe he is quite ready yet, Les. If I am correct, his larger device will require a significantly greater amount of energy. That fact should give us a bit more time and help us to locate him. That, at least, is my hope for how it will work itself out."

The car swerved a bit as Les stared too long at Urr. "I have to assume that the thought has occurred to you, that you could still avoid his trap. You could save yourself for another day by simply choosing to stay out of town for a while."

"Save myself," Urr said, "by letting him destroy the town." He smiled slightly. "Fedhisss knows me too well to consider that possibility." It was his turn to look at Les. "But the same reasoning applies to you, Les. You could drop me off in town and then return to the campus. Miss Sommers will be there, waiting for you."

Les felt his hands gripping the steering wheel more tightly. Shouldn't he follow Urr's suggestion? Wouldn't it be the reasonable thing to do? He laughed lightly, in spite of the tension he felt. "Save myself," he echoed Urr, "by letting him destroy the town." He continued driving.

"There's one other thing that puzzles me," Les said.

"Oh?" Urr said.

"Yes. It seems a rather obvious idea. Since you are both human beings for the moment, and apparently just as vulnerable as the rest of us, why doesn't Fedhisss get hold of a gun somewhere and simply walk up and shoot you, blow you away? End of pursuit."

"Yes," Urr nodded. "That would certainly be decisive. But Fedhisss would not be capable of doing it. Which brings me to a point that I must share with you now."

"No more touching!" Les said, leaning away from him.

"Not this time," Urr said. "A simple explanation will do. Fedhisss and I, within our elemental natures, are both unable to harm each other in any direct way. He has discovered during our voyage that he can inflict damage upon other life forms, but if he is planning to use his device to physically destroy me, he will have to find some way to get an intermediary to do it. That is why he gave the smaller device to the student in the laboratory."

"You think that's what he'll do, then? Try to trick somebody else into helping him?"

Urr considered. "I'm really not sure, Les. Knowing Fedhisss, I cannot rule out other possibilities that he will discover here. He could, for example, simply hire some local hit man and have me whacked."

Les showed his surprise. "You're sounding more and more like us, Urr."

"Not a compliment," Urr said. "My infusion included a sampling of your television programs. But the truth is that Fedhisss and I are both limited in that particular way. I could be faced with the same problem when confronting him. And here is where I must appeal to you."

"What do you mean?" Les said, glancing at him. "You expect me to do what? Physically assault him? Hit him over the head? A right cross to the jaw? Urr, I'm just not built that way. I haven't had to scuffle with anyone since I was a little kid back in my old neighborhood."

"No," Urr shook his head. "It was not a scuffle I had in mind. I will do my best to get Fedhisss to return to his vehicle and then to accompany me back to where we began our journey. But if he does not agree to do so, if, instead, as I believe he will do, he insists on continuing with his plans for a destructive act of much greater magnitude than we have yet seen, then I must ask you to serve as my intermediary."

"Which means?" Les said, frowning.

"That you take some step to radically disorganize the present containment of his consciousness."

"What are you saying?" Les said, unable to believe what he was hearing.

"It's a simple request," Urr said. "Decisive, as I earlier noted. And one that I am able, with my human capabilities, to consider. If it proves necessary, I want you to kill him."

39.

ENOUGH. I HAVE HAD enough of him and his pathetic ways. He should know by now that what I am doing is too important to be stopped. There are larger principles at stake here, the quality of life itself within this vast and still unsterilized universe.

We should not be wasting this much time. So much fuss over one insignificant planet infested with a peculiar life form plagued with such a devastating capability. Actually able to dissipate the organized energy of their own kind. Poof! And they are returned to the random driftings of the materials meandering through this haphazard universe, out of which, cell by cell, ironical forces have constructed their containments. Poof! Never to exist again. Why should it surprise me, then, that they so desperately attempt to delude themselves with their beliefs? Ultimate control over the workings of this world! And then? Transcendence! Eternal life!

Urr has allowed his consciousness to become riddled with the emotions of his present life form. Is that why I take so little pleasure in staying two steps ahead of him as I lure him on to that fateful moment when I will end his pursuit? It is proving to be a challenge that is hardly worthy of my many talents. He will find the small device that I left for him in the laboratory. He will examine it and discover that I need a greater source of power to achieve my goal. And then, once again, he will follow me.

Pagh! It is turning out all too easy!

40.

ANNE SAT AT HER desk in the lobby of the library, trying to fill out a number of book-order forms, but she was unable to concentrate on the task. Her mind was elsewhere, reaching out, trying to follow Les and Dr. Urr, who had left so quickly, and with Les so obviously disturbed. What was it that was upsetting him? Les had asked her to stay at the campus until he returned. Why? she wondered. What were they up to? And why had Dr. Urr avoided answering her?

It was wrong for them to have left her without any explanation. Did they expect her simply to wait there and not to worry? She was certainly worried about Les, she realized, but it was Dr. Urr who concerned her most, frightened her, really, with his strange abilities. How could he do things that were so unnatural, so...unearthly?

Normally, she would be thoughtful. She would do as Les had asked and stay at the campus. But now her emotions welled up confusedly within her, swirling around her thoughts of Les, mixing in her fear of Urr and his discomforting ways, until she felt the presence of some elemental threat that was circling around Les. And he was not aware that it was closing in on him. Oh, Les, be careful!

She looked over at Millie, who was leafing through a copy of a news magazine. "It's so terrible, Anne!" Millie held up the magazine. "Have you seen these pictures? All these children in Africa, starving. Those tiny little skinny bodies. And their eyes, Anne. Have you seen their eyes? And this one, with the flies on his face?"

Anne looked down at her desk, struggling mentally to block out her recollection of the photographs. She had looked at them earlier, but they had pierced through her with too much pain and confusion. The hopelessness in the faces of the children. Such an overwhelming grief. Who should be held responsible? How do you assign responsibility? It was beyond her capacity to understand. "Millie, I need to do something. Would you cover for me?" She left her desk without waiting for the answer and headed for the back exit.

"Sure, honey." Millie called after her, "If anybody asks, should I say where you are?"

"No, Millie," Anne called back. "I've got to see Les. It's important."

"Tell me something new," Millie said, smiling fondly at her.

Anne hurried out the exit and into the parking lot toward her car. Was it foolish of her to leave the campus this way, to hurry off in pursuit of Les just because of some vague fears?

As she reached her car, she paused a moment. The lot around her was full of vehicles, as it always was. Overhead, the rays of the sun were breaking through the lingering clouds. A slight breeze moving across the lot was cool on her face. She was standing in the midst of a familiar day, like so many days before. But she knew that there was something more. She could sense something more out there that was silently moving around her. From the first recollected glimmerings of her childhood consciousness, it had always been there, that intractable gathering of unseen forces that somehow came together, just beyond the edges of her awareness, to shape her world and her life toward its own impersonal ends. With every ounce of her emotional strength, she silently voiced her appeal to it.

"Please . Oh, please. Not this time. Don't take him away from me."

41.

LES CONTINUED SHAKING HIS head as they sped along the highway toward town. "No way, Urr. I just couldn't do it."

"Even if your own life depended on it?" Urr watched him closely.

It was a question that Les had grappled with earlier. What, after all, was he capable of doing if his own life was threatened, if he was certain that if he didn't act, he would surely die? But he had yet to come face to face with such a situation. How could he possibly know what was in him, part of his original equipment, so to speak, some evolutionary carry-over from prehistoric times that would compel him, without any thought, to take the life of anything or anyone threatening his, strike them senseless to the ground, smash their skulls in with a rock?

He shook his head again.

"And Miss Sommers' life?" Urr added.

Les winced. Score one for Urr, he thought. But he did not like the feeling that Urr was manipulating him.

"And everyone else within your town? The ones you know, and all the others? The individual cells of their bodies will shatter apart—"

"Why are you dropping this on me?" Les could feel his anger rising.

"I'm sorry, Les, but I have no alternative. There's not enough time to find someone else, to convince them that what I am saying is true, that if they—"

"All right, all right," Les said. "I get your point. Who would believe you?" He glanced at Urr, who was still watching him, and tried to smile. "A goofy-looking, weird-acting guy like you."

"Goofy-looking?" Urr returned his smile. "Miss Watson in the library did not think so."

"Millie?" Les laughed. "She'd eat you alive, Urr."

Urr nodded, and brightened at the thought.

As they neared the town, Urr pointed off to the string of pylons cutting across the countryside. "Those towers, Les, and the lines running between them, I assume they are electric transmission lines."

"That's right," Les said. "High-tension wires. They come in from somewhere up north, about fifty miles or so, where the main power plant is."

"And they supply the entire town with the electricity you use?"

"Yes," Les said.

"But they obviously have been strung to service a good number of other areas. Where and how is the electricity actually brought into your town?"

"As I recall," Les said, "I've passed a small substation on the edge of town. They tap into the high-tension lines at that point and from there distribute the power throughout this area. Do you think that's where Fedhisss will be heading?"

"Since the main plant is too far away, I would say it is a very likely possibility that we should check out."

"There's a road coming up that skirts the town. It will save us some time if we take it there."

"No," Urr said. "Go back into town. We have a crucial item that we must pick up first."

"Crucial item?" Les glanced at Urr. "What does that mean?"

"What you will need when we confront Fedhisss. The

means you will use to disorganize him."

Les frowned at him.

"A gun, obviously," Urr said. He looked at Les with a touch of exasperation. "Sometimes you make me wonder if you're really human."

42.

I NOTE HERE THAT I remain somewhat perplexed by the deeper magma of human emotions, still being moved by ancient forces beneath the shallow streams of their conscious thoughts. It can suddenly erupt without warning in the midst of any rational moment, spewing forth a searing heat and blinding smoke. And then they can become unpredictably dangerous, for within this lower level lurks the destroyer of its own species.

Fedhisss will certainly explore this area of their nature as he seeks for an appropriate intermediary.

In response, I continue to delve more deeply into that darkened region within Les, searching for a counteracting killer.

43.

LES PULLED IN AND parked beside the building where he had his apartment. "I don't even know if he's here," Les said. "What do I tell him if he is?"

"Whatever you think is appropriate," Urr said. "What do people usually say when they want to borrow a gun?"

"How would I know?" Les said, shrugging slightly. "I've never borrowed a gun before." He looked at the house, considering what to say. "Excuse me, Mike. Do you have a spare gun I could borrow? My friend here has somebody that he would like me to shoot."

Urr nodded. "Not bad. Give it a try."

"Sure," Les said, getting out of the car. Urr followed him to the front steps and then waited as he went up and rang the bell. After a few moments, as Les was about to turn and leave, Mike came to the door, yawning and looking a bit bleary-eyed. "Les," he said, trying to shake himself awake. "You caught me in the middle of a nap. What can I do for you?"

"I'm sorry, Mike. Bad timing. But I was wondering if it would be possible for me to borrow one of your guns for a couple of hours."

"One of my guns?" Mike looked amused. "You, of all people, Les. What do you need with a gun?"

"It's not me," Les said, looking somewhat uncomfortable as he dredged up an explanation. "We're visiting a friend to the north of town, and he's got a sick raccoon in his yard. It looks like it's about to die, but it seems to be in a lot of pain, and I don't want it to suffer any longer."

"You want to put it out of its misery." Mike gave it some thought, and then nodded slowly. "Hate to see anything suffer myself. All right, I think I have a handgun that I could let you have for that," he smiled at Les, "so long as you don't shoot yourself in the foot."

"I'll be careful," Les said, but with the passing thought that his foot could easily be in danger.

"Hang on a moment, and I'll get it." He went back into his house. After what seemed to be too long a wait, he returned with a small revolver. "I've loaded it for you, Les. And the safety's on. Here." He demonstrated for Les. "Off." *Click.* "On." *Click.* "Please keep it on until you're ready to shoot, and then put it on again right after you shoot. Will you do that, Les? Will you promise me?" He took a long look at Les. He appeared to be having second thoughts.

"Of course," Les said. "And I really thank you. We'll be very careful with this." He reached out for the revolver, not quite sure how to take hold of it, but then he remembered a television program he had recently seen. The detective had held his gun upright, with his straightened index finger kept safely on the side of the trigger guard, not curled around the trigger. Les grasped the revolver that way and glanced at Mike, who nodded his approval and looked somewhat relieved.

Les went down off the porch, the gun still held up at attention, as he and Urr made their way back to the car. When they had both entered the vehicle, Les sat there a moment, wondering what he should do with the gun so that he could drive. Urr saw his hesitation. "Put it in your belt, or in your pocket."

Les tried sticking the revolver into the front of his belt, but he had visions of it falling down through his pants leg when he got out of the car. Or it might go off as he drove along and do

146

irreparable damage to parts of him that he would just as soon avoid shooting. He put the revolver in his right pants-pocket, feeling its weight on his leg, uncomfortable with the sense of it shifting around slightly as he moved to start the car.

He was backing out toward the street when he saw Anne's car pull in behind him. "Oh, no," he said. "Anne. Why couldn't she do as I asked?" He stopped his car abruptly, and they both got out, walking back to speak with her. He was about to say something harsh, when he saw the concerned look on her face.

"I'm sorry, Les. I don't mean to pry." She kept glancing at Urr, who was standing just behind Les. "But I was anxious about you, and I couldn't understand why you wouldn't talk with me earlier." Another glance at Urr. "Whatever it is that's troubling you, would you like to talk with me privately about it?"

"A reasonable request," Urr said from behind Les. "But we are a bit pressed for time. May I recommend that Miss Sommers accompany us?"

"No!" Les said. "I don't want her involved in this!"

"She's already involved. You know that. Everyone here in the town is."

"In what, Les?" Her look was tinged again with a pained confusion. "What is it that you're doing?"

"Think for a moment, Les," Urr said. "If we succeed in stopping Fedhisss, then everything will be fine, and you two can go on with your lives. But if he succeeds in destroying us, then it simply won't matter whether any one of us survives. It would be, at best, a delayed destruction."

"Stop it!" Anne cried out with an anguished voice. "Stop this kind of talk!" She turned pleadingly to Les. "It just isn't fair. You can't leave me this way. What is it you're doing, Les, that could get you hurt, that could get you...destroyed." She struggled to say the word, as though it were too unbelievable to express.

Les considered Urr's argument and Anne's state of mind. "All right," he said. "Then you'd better come with us, Anne. But we've got to hurry. We're running out of time. I'll explain on the way."

He opened her car door and took her hand to help her out. Standing in front of her, still holding her hand, he could not help admiring her. A lovely woman who loved him. She had given him her trust and now deserved his in return. But he could also see in her upturned look the bright and intelligent woman who was watching him closely now.

"You'll never believe it," he said.

44.

"Oh, Les." She looked embarrassed for him. "You can't be serious."

"I know how it sounds, Anne, but, believe me, it's true. He showed me his spaceship."

They were nearing the substation at the north edge of town by the time Les had finished his story. Sitting quietly beside him on the front seat of the car, she had listened carefully to everything he said. "His spaceship," she repeated, as though speaking sympathetically to a small child desperately trying to tell a large fib. "And why did he involve you in all of this?"

"So that I would help him to stop Fedhisss, who intends to destroy all life forms on this planet." Les grimaced and shook his head. "I know it sounds crazy, Anne. But remember the tornado that touched down, and the physics book he put in your mind, and my awareness of your childhood loss. How would you explain those things?"

She turned then to look at Urr, who was in the back seat, but his face, as usual, was expressionless as he returned her look. "What have you done to him," she said, "to make him believe in such terrible lies?" He was a man who clearly confused her, she realized. But why was he doing this? What were his intentions? And was he in some way dangerous? "You're clever, I know. I've seen that. And you have some unaccountably strange ways about you." She felt a shiver as she recalled them. "But I don't yet understand what you are up to."

"I'm trying to help you," Urr said.

"You've told me that before," Anne said. "But do you think it's a help to put such ideas into Les's mind?"

"Yes, I do," Urr said, "if they're true."

It was his calmness that disturbed her most, the sense he gave of there being no question that what he said was obviously so. And how, indeed, as Les had asked, would she explain his puzzling ways?

"No!" she shook her head firmly. "I will not fall for your game, whatever it is."

Urr smiled slightly. "I did not expect you to do so, Miss Sommers. You have a distinctive mind of your own. It will let you decide for yourself. But, here, we have reached the substation. We must turn our thoughts elsewhere now."

Les pulled off the road and parked.

"Anne, please, stay in the car," he said.

She shook her head again. "I can't do that, Les. I'm sorry. Whatever is going on here, I want to see for myself."

Held for a moment by her determination, admiring the strength of it, he relented and smiled slightly. "All right," he said. "I understand."

The three of them got out of the car and slowly, cautiously made their way toward the substation, as Urr and Les looked around the grounds for any signs of Fedhisss.

The substation was bordered by a high, rectangular, chain-link fence. There was a gate through the fence which was normally chained and padlocked. The chain had been un-wrapped from the gate, and the padlock hung open. Inside the fence, on all sides, was a wide area of cleared ground designed to keep the center of the substation isolated from anyone outside of the fence. In the center, jutting well above

the height of the fence, and built over two massive trans-
formers, was an extensive framework of steel beams that
were bristling with large, electrical connectors. A sign on
the fence, in bright red letters, read, "Danger High Voltage."

Glancing up, Anne was the first to see him. "Look!" she
cried, amazed at the sight.

Halfway up the structure on one of the steel beams, between two of the many electrical conductors studding the
beam, Fedhisss sat with his feet dangling comfortably beneath him. Next to him on the beam was a metallic box with
two wires looping down from the rear and back up to two
of the nearby connectors. A circular opening on the front of
the box was pointed in the direction of the gate, which also
faced toward the town.

"Welcome!" Fedhisss called down to them, looking delighted. Seated as he was among the electrical connectors, in
danger of being electrocuted by the slightest wrong move, he
appeared to be oblivious to his precarious position. "Welcome
one and all." He opened his arms, as though to take them in.

Wondering what they should do, Les glanced at Urr, who
appeared to be perplexed as he continued looking around
the grounds and off to each side, as though expecting to
find someone else. The intermediary, Les remembered. He
then turned to Anne and saw the confusion flooding her
face as she looked back and forth again and again from Urr
to Fedhisss. "They're identical," she said, struggling to understand. She turned to Les with widened eyes. "But that
doesn't mean...." Her resistance strengthened. "He could
be just a twin!"

Les reached out and took her hand, holding it firmly as he
turned back to face Fedhisss up on the framework.

"Perhaps," Fedhisss said, "I should quickly mention that
if you try to approach me, Urr, or if any of you attempts to

harm me in any way, I will throw this lever on the side of my little accomplishment here," he patted the metallic box next to him, "and your town will be—What should I say? Your town will be blown away! By the next passing breeze!" He smiled gleefully, obviously enjoying himself. "Isn't that remarkable?"

"But we're standing in that path," Les said, frowning and turning to Urr. "I thought you said that he could not directly harm you. If he sets that thing off...."

"An excellent question," Fedhisss said. "But since I am up here high enough, I can focus it on the town, so it will pass over you. I wouldn't, I couldn't, hurt my old friend Urr." As he stared at Urr, a visible sense of menace came into his face. "My old, deluded, distorted friend Urr."

"What is it," Urr said, his expression now calm, "that you intend to do next?"

"Ah," Fedhisss said. "Now that will be the interesting part. But first I must test my little device here. What if it didn't work? Now that would prove rather troublesome, wouldn't it?" He reached for the box.

"Test it?" Les cried out. "What do you mean, test it?"

"No need to worry...yet," said Fedhisss, smiling down at Les. "I'll be pointing it away from your town, out into the woods over there, and I will not be using its full power. Just a little test, so we can all be certain that it will work. Doesn't that make sense?" He swiveled the box to one side, aiming it towards the woods, and pressed the lever on its side partially down.

With a deafening *whooosh* that startled all of them, trees and undergrowth in the distant woods shattered before their eyes. Every leaf and grassblade, birds among the branches, earthworms in the dirt—whatever life forms had been alive within the irradiated area—had instantaneously burst outward as a darkening mist moving among and above the trees, forming into a canopy that rose and slowed and then hovered over a now visible swath of destruction cutting through the woods.

They all stood transfixed as the mist thinned and began to drift away with a passing breeze.

Fedhisss wiggled his feet in delight. "Isn't that remarkable?"

"My God," Anne said softly. Her resistance to Les's outlandish story, which she had persistently maintained up to this very moment, completely collapsed now. "Oh, Les," she said turning to him. "I can't believe it. It's true, isn't it? They're not from here."

"Delightful!" Fedhisss was still enjoying the sight of the woods. "Every shattering is so beautiful!" He looked down at the three of them. "So very beautiful. Don't you agree?"

Anne squeezed Les's hand as another realization chilled her to the bone. "And that one, up there. He's mad, isn't he?" She struggled to resist the wave of despair that almost overwhelmed her.

45.

"Impressive," Urr said, speaking up to Fedhisss. "If your intention was to impress us, then you have succeeded. But my question nevertheless remains unanswered. What is it that you intend to do next?"

"Ah, yes," Fedhisss said, as he repositioned the metallic box to face toward the town again. "The more interesting part of what I have in mind. You know that I am fair and honest about everything I do, Urr, and I want to be fair about this matter, too. So I am going to offer your two acquaintances the opportunity to save their town. Certainly, I cannot be more fair than that."

"My two acquaintances," Urr said, looking at them. "Les and Miss Sommers. Are they an appropriate pair to confront you in any contest you would devise? I fail to see the fairness here."

"Yes," Fedhisss said, musing for a moment. "I have given that matter a great deal of thought, and here is what I have decided. I will pose three *earthly* questions to them, and if they are able to answer the questions correctly, then I will pack my bag and, with your concurrence, we will both depart this planet, never to return. We can then continue our little disagreement within some other region of the universe."

"What satisfaction could you possibly derive from showing off your superiority to two human beings?"

"Oh, Urr, you disappoint me again. It's getting to be a habit, isn't it? What I am doing here is not so sordid as that. There is a much greater issue before us, the quality of life itself."

"We've been over that issue before," Urr said. "If you believe that you are right, and you are determined to pursue your course of action, then return with me now, so that we can both present our views to the Circle. If you are so indisputably convinced of your position, then you should have no problem in returning to defend it. Let them decide, Fedhisss. I will abide by their decision."

"No, Urr." Fedhisss scowled at him. "I know what I am doing. Now you will abide by my decision. We will proceed as I have just described, or without any further hesitation, I will uninfest this town." He reached out and took hold of the lever on the side of the metallic box.

"All right," said Urr. "Then proceed as you wish."

"Excellent," Fedhisss said, dropping his hand. "And what could be a more fair sampling for this little gathering? A man with an intellect riddled with emotions. And a woman with emotions riddled with intellect." His face grew sober as he studied each of them. "I am assuming that you understand the issue before us. It is a question of survival. Not simply your own." He waved his hand, as though brushing aside a bit of dust. "But of all the peculiar varieties of enfeebled consciousness that have emerged within the crudely constructed life forms that are found here on this planet."

"If you have already prejudged us," Les said, feeling his irritation rising, "then I, too, fail to see the fairness."

Fedhisss ignored the remark as he looked down upon Les and Anne. "Shall we begin now?" He raised his eyebrows. "Do I have your attention?"

Les glanced at Urr, who shrugged slightly. "I see no clear alternative at this point, if you wish to save your town."

As she listened to Fedhisss and Urr, Anne's grip on Les's

hand had tightened again until he finally winced. "We've got to go for help, Les. There are thousands of people living in town. We've got to stop him."

"The question," Les said, "is how? You've seen what he can do with the device. He has the ability to end all of our lives. And apparently he's prepared to do so."

"Then we'll go for the police," Anne said, her desperation showing now. "It's not that far back into town."

She started to pull him toward the car, but he held his ground, shaking his head. "Before we could even reach the car, there would be no one left in town to go to, the police or anyone else." She stared at him, the stress in her growing until she was on the point of tears.

He reached out and cupped her face in his hands, holding her imploring look until she could see what he was now offering her. It was the only thing, under the immediate threat, that he was sure he had left to offer, the depth of love he felt for her. He watched her calming herself as she accepted it.

"You are taxing my patience," Fedhisss said.

"Then begin your little game," Les said, turning to him. "And we'll see what kind of creature you really are."

"And after each of your questions," Anne spoke up, "we reserve the right to ask you one in return."

Les looked at her, surprised. "What have you got in mind?"

"I have no idea," she said.

"Excellent!" Fedhisss seemed delighted by Anne's challenge. "A mutual evaluation! Three questions to determine which of us deserves to survive!" He wiggled his feet beneath the steel beam, unable to contain his pleasure. "Shall we proceed then?"

His gleeful expression suddenly darkened. "Question one."

46.

SITTING ABOVE THEM ON the steel beam, Fedhisss looked down upon Les and Anne, as though they were specimens recently gathered that needed now to be pinned to a board. "Tell me," he said. He slowly considered each of them, his eyes touched by a mocking amusement. "Among all of your earthly life forms, what creature goes on four feet in the morning, two feet at noonday, and three feet in the evening?"

Watching him closely, Les raised his eyebrows, and then almost laughed aloud. "That's your first question?"

"It is," said Fedhisss. "And your answer?"

Both Les and Anne knew the answer from their own past readings, and Urr, by touching into them, had gathered the answer from them. Les turned to Urr. "Is he serious?"

"Oh, yes," Urr said.

"Then what is he up to?"

Urr continued to study Fedhisss, who was looking only at Les and Anne, apparently unwilling to recognize Urr's presence. "We'll know very soon," Urr said.

"Must you persist in testing my good nature?" Fedhisss offered them an exaggerated look of strained patience. "I have asked you for your answer."

"All right," Les said, facing him again. "Your question is a well-known riddle that was posed by the Sphinx to Oedipus. If Oedipus did not answer correctly, the Sphinx would devour him."

The image appeared to excite Fedhisss. "Yes," he said, prolonging the sibilant sound.

Les had never seen such a malevolent look. It held him for a moment before he could speak. "Oedipus replied that the subject of the riddle was a man, who, as a baby at the beginning of life, crawls on all fours, and at the noon of life walks upright, and then, as an old man with a cane, makes his way near the end of life."

Fedhisss paused a moment, and then shook his head slightly.

"The answer is correct!" Les protested.

"Of course, it's correct," Fedhisss said. "I truly wish it weren't."

"Yes," Les said. "I'll bet you do."

"Oh, don't misunderstand me." Fedhisss swung his feet under the beam as he looked out above them toward the town. "It would have been such a pleasure to discover an advanced form of life on this planet, a form that I could admire for the quality of its existence. But you have just characterized your species as being a pathetically transitory form. You begin in a state of prolonged helplessness, crawling on the ground like the lower forms out of which you have evolved. Then you straighten up for the briefest moment to take a quick, confusing look around you at your deficient world, after which you rapidly degenerate into a state of slobbering dissolution. A terminal state. Poof! And you're gone forever." Slowly, with a look of disgust on his face, he shook his head again.

Anne spoke up. "What a distorted impression! You recognize only the negative side of our lives. If that is the case, then I, too, fail to see the fairness of your assuming that you can sit in judgment of us."

Fedhisss appeared to ignore her remarks. "You said that you had a question in return for each of mine. Proceed."

"I will," she said. "Tell me this. To what degree are you aware of the complexities of human nature?"

"My awareness of the complexities of human nature, as you put it, extends well beyond that achieved by yourself. And what am I to make of that?" Fedhisss looked off to one side, as though bored and searching for some distraction. "The nature of a rabbit, as I am also aware, contains its own degree of complexity, but that does not stop you from serving up your rabbit stew. Or your roast beef. Or your ham and eggs. Or whatever other containments of consciousness you choose to disorganize and then devour to maintain your own unfortunate existence."

Gripping the edges of the steel beam, he leaned down toward them. "My turn now." His eyes, as he stared at them, were like two chips of anthracite coal. They smoldered for a moment and then flared. "Question number two."

47.

ONCE AGAIN, BEFORE HE spoke, he looked at Les and Anne, frowning, as though he were having some difficulty in understanding them. Why did such a deplorable life form wish to survive? "Starting with the closest," he said, "can you tell me the names of the nine planets that orbit your sun?"

Les appeared to be troubled by the question, but Anne moved closer to him and spoke softly. "I know that answer. It was in the physics book that Dr. Urr gave me. Shall I tell him?"

It was Les's turn to calm his own mounting tension. He reached up to stroke her cheek and suddenly, to his surprise, found that he was capable of touching within her, deeper than the sensory surface of her flesh, to the woman existing as a presence in the body. Suddenly, he became aware that his own interior life, which he had guarded unrelentingly for so long against any intrusions, was resonating now in harmony with hers, as when a struck bell pealing across the intervening air causes a distant bell to vibrate responsively. For an endless second, a shiver of pleasure ran through him.

Then, as he lowered his hand, he was aware again of standing by the gate beside Anne and Urr, with Fedhisss waiting for their answer. "Tell him," he said.

Turning to Fedhisss, Anne spoke slowly and calmly. "Mercury, Venus, Earth, Mars, Jupiter, Saturn, Uranus, Neptune, and Pluto." She waited for his response.

Fedhisss considered her for a moment before replying.

"Peculiar, isn't it, that only Earth is not named for one of your multitude of gods, especially when you believed for so many years that the entire universe revolved around it. But wait!" He brightened and held up his finger, in a mock display of achieving some illuminating insight. "I believe I know the reason for that! It was not the Earth that the universe revolved around. It was you! And all the other passing human beings who placed themselves at the center of the universe as their lives briefly flickered and then faded to nothing." He paused, as though in awe. "Isn't that remarkable?" And then the brightness left his face. "But even that was not enough for you. You then had to imagine a god or two who not only had brought into existence this vast and still mysterious universe, but who also considered you, each and every one of you, to be that god's most illustrious creation and the eternal center of its concern." The darkness in his look deepened. "But even that was not enough. You then had to believe that you, and only you, were the elite, the elected, the chosen ones that the god treasured above all other human beings, the precious ones whose enemies the god would confound and punish by means of your bloody hands, casting all who did not share your beliefs into hellish fires, as the god gently lifted you, the jewels of his creation, up to eternal bliss. What an astonishing arrogance!" His face twisted in repugnance. "To assume that you were the highest form of life within the entire universe. Higher even than I! It's so distasteful!" His features twisted even further. "So repulsive!"

As the three of them stood by the gate to the substation, watching Fedhisss up on the beam going through his contorted reactions, Les felt a slight breeze on his face and glanced up at the sky, where a scattering of feathery white clouds were drifting overhead. He felt the peaceful sense they gave off. Beautiful day, he thought, and almost smiled, before he glanced down again to recognize the sheer madness, as Anne had named it, of what was going on here.

He slipped his hand into his pocket and gripped the revolver. Should he attempt to kill the man now? At the cost of the entire town? But if the man was not stopped here, regardless of the immediate cost, what would he go on to do beyond this point? Was it really possible that this single being, sitting there so casually dangling his legs, could wreak havoc around the entire planet, uninfest it, as he said, of all its many life forms? Unbelievable.

But the test of the device beside Fedhisss was still burnt into Les's mind. And another memory came to him, the time that Urr had touched into him to share with him a view of the last planet the two of them had visited, and the breathtaking devastation that Fedhisss had left behind there, the sense of an elemental destruction, the ominous absence of all life. Unbelievable?

"Again!' Fedhisss spoke down to them from his perch. "Once again you prolong things! Must you always do so? Another deplorable human characteristic. It is time for your second question."

Les turned to Urr. "Any suggestions?"

Urr shook his head. "But I believe that I know now where he is heading. I would advise you simply to continue playing his game, and we'll see if I am right."

Les turned reluctantly back to face Fedhisss. He had little hope of being able to reason with the man, but saw no other option for the moment to following Urr's advice. "Tell me then," he said, looking up at Fedhisss. "Since you have illustrated for us once again the blatant bias you display in your one-sided view of us, can you give me a clear and effective example of something *positive* about us?"

Fedhisss considered the question and then smiled cheerfully as a thought occurred to him. "Yes! Something positive. I can answer that. It's an obvious point, if you are able to judge it objectively. I'm referring to the brevity of your existence, the fact that you are not around that long to suffer the many afflictions to which you are vulnerable, and that you do not have much time to inflict your natures upon each other and the other life forms here. Your consciousness flickers for the briefest of moments, and then quickly withers. And then you die. A blessing, when you think about it. Don't you agree?"

Les shook his head slowly. The man was obviously intent on distorting everything they said. "Once again, you misrepresent a central feature of our lives. Yes, from your viewpoint, we do have a brief existence, but that very brevity enhances the appreciation we have for life in ways that you apparently are unable to comprehend. There are so many moments in our lives that become intensely precious to us, simply because we know that they will not stay. They can be common, everyday moments, like a walk on a foggy beach in the early morning as the sky begins to clear. Or a calm sunset of soft colors that spread out to fill the sky, overwhelming your senses, before they suddenly, poignantly, evaporate to gray. Or gently touching the cheek of a woman you deeply love, and yearning for that exquisitely fragile moment to last forever."

Anne moved closer and leaned softly against him.

Les looked with a new and saddened interest at Fedhisss. "Across the seemingly limitless span of your own existence, have you ever experienced such a moment?" He tried to look into Fedhisss, to see behind his mocking expression. "I doubt if you are capable of it. And so I must judge your nature to be inadequate and out of place within a constantly evolving universe."

Urr smiled gently at Les and began slowly to clap his hands, a response which seemed only to irritate Fedhiss, who strengthened his mocking look, almost sneering down at them. "Once again, I am truly amazed at the capacity of a human being to delude himself. Do you seriously expect me to accept the view that your appreciation of existence is enhanced because you live so shortly? With that line of reasoning, I could argue that I am about to raise the appreciation level of everyone living in your town. Ha!" He threw his head back as he laughed and closed his eyes, almost losing his balance on the beam. He recovered, and, after settling himself again on his perch, he casually reached over and put his hand on the top of the metallic box beside him, taunting them with the gesture as he looked down at the three of them.

Les spoke up quickly. "We're playing by your rules, aren't we? As I recall, you said that if we answered your three questions correctly, you would leave this planet unharmed and never return." Les turned to Urr and kept his voice raised, wanting to put Fedhisss on the spot in front of Urr. "Does his word have any weight, Urr? Can he be trusted to do what he says?"

"Oh, yes," Urr said. "Whatever else he may do, you can believe him when he gives his word."

"Of course," said Fedhisss, with an irritating twitch, as though the issue were not worth discussing.

"All right," said Les. "Then since we have correctly answered your first two questions, regardless of your biased responses to them, you must honor your word and leave this planet if we correctly answer the third."

"Indeed," said Fedhisss. "Only one to go." Slowly, reluctantly, he took his hand back away from the metallic box and turned to face Les again.

48.

"Now LET ME SEE," Fedhisss said, stroking his chin. "What should I ask you for the final question? What could I possibly ask you that would clarify the issue before us? Hmmm." He put his chin in his right hand and then rested his right elbow on his left leg, an obvious parody of Rodin's statue *The Thinker*.

"Who is delaying now?" Les said, anxious and wanting to hear the question.

"I couldn't resist it," Fedhisss said, smiling. "Another interesting human characteristic. You apparently are unable to think without contorting your body into peculiar positions. Oh, well. Let us proceed."

Settling himself on the beam again, he stared now at Les, and then at Anne, as though he were taking his last look, and wanted to remember it. "I pose this question to both of you," he said. "Listen very carefully. If we gathered all of the evidence available to this date regarding the nature and actions of your species, the history of your presence upon the surface of this planet, and we separated that evidence into what has been good about you and what has been bad, and then placed each side on a chemist's balancing scales...." He paused a moment to give them time to mentally do what he was directing. "This, then, is my final question to the two of you. If Urr were now to be given the responsibility of judging you objectively, which way would he see the scales tip? For or against your existence as a distinctive life form?"

Surprised by the question, Les brightened and turned quickly to look at Urr, seeking for some indication that Urr would certainly support them. But Urr's face was again without expression. His eyes, resting now on Les, did not hold any evident recognition. Urr was now the calm and objective observer, waiting patiently to hear Les's answer.

Les turned to Anne, smiling slightly. "We should be all right."

"Are you sure?" she said, glancing at Urr. "He troubles me, Les. He always has. Both of them They're different from us. How do we know what he really thinks?"

Les clung firmly to his own hope. "Well, there's only one way to find out, isn't there?"

"Yes," she said, reaching out to touch his arm, needing to reassure herself that this wasn't just some foolish dream swirling around her from which she would soon awaken. "You know him better than I do, Les. I'll leave it up to you. Whatever you believe the truth to be, that's what you should tell him."

He put his hand over hers and kept it there, not wanting to lose her touch. Finally, he nodded and looked up toward Fedhisss.

"I begin my answer," he said, raising his voice again, "by noting that we are not a simple species, as you would like to make us out. As a life form, I do not deny that we are a paradox. But perhaps it is because we have emerged within a paradoxical world. How else are we to judge a world that apparently supports our existence, since we are, after all, here, while persistently heaping afflictions upon us and throwing roadblocks up in our way? In an often fearful and confusing state, our species has had to struggle for its survival across too many centuries. But as we have struggled, we have also sought to give meaning to our lives, some purpose that would allow us to believe we were more than just some cosmic backwater accident. Yes, as you have already remarked, we have all too often deluded ourselves, with our myths and our religions," he glanced at Urr, "and even with our sciences. You would consider them delusions born out of our ignorance and dismiss them with scorn. But I would not forget that we live in a paradoxical world, and in such a world our ignorance also has a value that we recognize. Throughout our history, as we tried to comprehend some purpose behind the pains and the sufferings of our existence, our ignorance has led us to the enliving of our imaginations, allowing us to fashion out of the very confusion and the perplexities surrounding us our greatest works of literature and art and music. They have served us well as artistic and moral signposts, enticing us to continue moving forward toward something that we still believe is awaiting us in our future, something that will finally unravel for us the paradoxical nature of our world.

"Is it simply a deluding ignorance? Whatever the case, it has kept us moving together, somewhat more hopefully and cooperatively, through dire circumstances over which we had no control. And it has brought us now to our present state of existence.

"Across our history, I cannot deny the persistent presence of man's inhumanity to man, our many hurtful acts, our cruelties, our senseless destructions. But if you are looking for the cause of them, then turn again to that ignorance in us that you deplore, and join it to the fear we felt, and have not handled at all well, in discovering how vulnerable we had been left in a world of impersonal and potentially deadly forces.

"But now we have a glimmering of hope. We are beginning to reach a new level as we emerge out of that fearful side of our lives, a level that is allowing us, not only to better understand and accept each other, but actually to reach out to each other, or should I say to touch each other, or better still, to touch into each other."

Les paused for a moment as he realized that he was no longer speaking to Fedhisss. It was Urr that he was now directing his words to, Urr who would now decide their fate. Les turned and held Urr's gaze, looking again for some sign, smiling softly at him as he felt the friendship that had grown between them. "In the very short time that you have been here, you have learned a great deal about us, not only about the troublesome aspects of our past, but also the potential we now possess to develop into a higher life form that can earn your respect. Are you willing to recognize where we are now? Are you willing to take our potential into account?"

When he saw Urr pensively frown, considering his remarks, and could find no trace of anything negative in Urr's expression. Les felt a surge of hope move through him.

"Then this is my answer," he said, turning to speak to Fedhisss again. "I believe that Urr would see the scales tip in our favor."

Sitting up on the steel beam, watching Les closely, Fedhisss smiled down at him and began to clap his hands slowly in imitation of Urr's earlier gesture. "Oh, Urr, wasn't that a lovely speech? Grandiloquent! It brought me near to tears, as I'm sure it did to you." He brushed his fingers under each of his eyes. "Now all we need to do is hear your decision."

Straightening himself on the steel beam, he silently regarded Urr. "Tell us," he said. His voice was tinged now with something that Les couldn't identify, something personal between Fedhisss and Urr, a tone of challenge, perhaps, as Fedhisss spoke. "How would you judge the weight of the evidence we have gathered regarding the existence of this species? For? Or against?"

Urr continued to look at Fedhisss, their eyes locked in the challenge that Fedhisss was posing. Les could sense the almost palpable struggle that was going on between them, the tension that was steadily rising as each held his own unwavering gaze, both indomitably determined to prevail in their contest of wills. "Your answer, Urr." Fedhisss was insistent now. "Your honest and objective answer."

The words made Urr frown again, and he dropped his eyes. He continued looking down as he spoke. "Objectively, as I consider the evidence...." He turned to look at Les and Anne, his features shaped by sadness and regret. "The scales would tip against them."

Shocked, Les cried out his disbelief. "Urr!"

"Ha!" said Fedhisss, his face brightening with glee. "How unfortunate! Your third answer. It's wrong!" He reached for the lever on the box beside him.

"No!" Anne cried. "Wait! You can't do that!"

"Oh, but I can," Fedhisss said, looking calmly down at her as he took hold of the lever.

49.

"ARENT YOU FORGETTING SOMETHING?" Les said, trying to keep his stress under control. "You haven't heard our third question yet!"

Fedhisss hesitated. "What's the point? Your answer was wrong."

"The point," Les said, "is this. You say you have a cause that you are determined to pursue. Across our existence here on this planet, members of our species have died for a good many causes. Tell me, Fedhisss." Les slipped his hand into his pocket. "Are you willing to die for your cause?" He brought the revolver out and clicked off the safety. Steadying it in both hands held out before him, he clicked back the hammer and aimed at Fedhisss. "Because, as soon as you move that lever, I will shoot you. I'll kill you." He groped for the right words among the things that Urr had told him, trying to get through to Fedhisss. "I'll disorganize the present containment of your consciousness, and terminate your existence."

Anne was startled by the sight of the gun. She stared, speechless, at Les, trying to see in his face if he would actually use it, looking now with some confusion at a part of Les that she had not seen before.

"My, my," Fedhisss said, keeping his hand on the lever. "I'll have to think about that a moment."

Les kept the revolver aimed at Fedhisss, trying not to look away as he spoke. "What have you done here, Urr?"

"I'm truly sorry, Les. But I had no alternative. I had to answer objectively."

"So you don't think we should survive," Les said, a trace of bitterness in his voice.

"It was the way he worded the question, Les. It was not your potential he asked me to judge. It was the history of your species to this point. I could not ignore what human beings have already done to each other, or your destructive use of a multitude of other life forms. You are not even very well constructed yet as a containment of consciousness. Still too vulnerable to dissolution. It has left you, as you have said yourself, in a persistently fearful state that has caused you to do too many terrible things." He paused as he saw the hurt looks on both of their faces. "But I do sincerely believe in your potential, Les. I have watched you and Miss Sommers closely, touching into each of you. You two are representative of the promising, but still untested, potential of your species. I would willingly give you, at this time, the benefit of all of my doubts. But that was not what Fedhisss asked me to judge. He knew what my response would be before he posed his question. And he counted on our friendship to mislead you into your wrong answer."

Les took it all in, still holding the gun on Fedhisss. "So where does that leave us? Where do we go from here?"

"Apparently," Urr said, "that will now be up to what Fedhisss decides. Is he willing to destroy your town as the final act of his own existence?" They all waited, watching Fedhisss. Les wondered if he should fire the revolver, try for a lucky shot that would knock Fedhisss off the beam before he could act. But Fedhisss was holding firmly onto the lever.

"My final act..." Fedhisss mused. "I see no alternative. If I am not to consider myself a hypocrite, mouthing beliefs that I am not willing to support with my very existence, then I must continue with my decision to uninfest this area. There will be others, I am sure, who will carry on after me, others who will look to me, admire me, for my unswerving commitment to raise the quality of their existence." He bent over slightly, looking down at his hand on the lever.

Les felt his grip on the pistol tighten. He curled his finger around the trigger, waiting tensely for the moment to fire.

"Unless..." Fedhisss said, looking up at them, as though a thought had just occurred to him. He turned to Les. "Tell me, would you really be willing to kill in order to save your species from extinction?"

"Apparently so," Les said grimly, "since I'm about to do it."

"Not that your answer surprises me, after seeing what a murderous lot you are. But if you had the opportunity, since you recognize now that Urr and I do not belong here, would you be willing to kill us both to rid your planet, now and forever, of the threat you face?"

Anne moved closer and spoke softly. "Be careful, Les. He can't be trusted."

"Why do you ask?" he said to Fedhisss.

"Because I will make you an offer now that will be only half as murderous. Once again, I will give you my word that I will leave this planet unharmed, never to return. All you have to do to bring that about is simply to kill Urr."

Fedhisss saw the shock on their faces. "Think a moment about Urr and me. We are outsiders who have come here uninvited. Our coming has placed your species, and indeed all of the life forms here, under the threat of extinction. You can do away with that threat from us forever, simply by re-moving one of us. Urr's life for all of the life forms existing on this planet. That strikes me as more than a reasonable offer."

"Clever," Urr said. "You were always very clever, Fedhisss. Your challenge to Les and Miss Sommers. It was not to give them a chance to save their town. It was designed from the beginning to stop me, to end my pursuit of you, by forcing Les to act as your intermediary."

The gun that Les was holding up with his two hands before him, pointed steadily at Fedhisss, was beginning to feel heavy now. He lowered it somewhat and brought his elbows back to his body to ease the weight, still ready to fire, though, if necessary. He could not prevent himself from glancing at Urr, who was still watching Fedhisss. The offer that Fedhisss had made was crazy, but Urr had confirmed that his word could be trusted, that he would do what he said. Les would be trading the life of one intruder, an alien from God knows where, for the thousands of lives within his town, and the permanent removal of the threat to his entire world in the future. Good Lord! What should he do?

The strain on Les's face revealed his inner conflict.

Urr looked sympathetically at Les. "I have placed you in an awkward position," he said. "It was not my intention to do so, and I must accept responsibility for it." He nodded to himself and, with a calm voice, revealed his decision. "You may shoot me now, Les."

"What?" Les couldn't believe that he had heard him correctly.

"You have no alternative," Urr said. "If you think the matter through reasonably, you will see that Fedhisss has offered you a solution to the difficulties we have brought you. A single bullet, well aimed, will bring about what Fedhisss desires, the termination of my existence. He will then do as he has told you. He will leave your planet unharmed. Isn't that exactly what you want to happen?"

"Are you telling me," Les said, still disbelieving, "that you *want* me to shoot you?"

Urr smiled slightly. "I'm not excited about the idea. But we both can recognize that Fedhisss has left us with only one choice. My life, or the thousands of lives existing throughout your town. It's a clear and rational choice, Les. Why do you hesitate?"

"Yes, indeed!" Fedhisss called down impatiently from his perch. "It's time for you to act. You have no other choice."

Still confused and groping for some sense of what he should do, Les looked back and forth at Fedhisss and Urr, with the gun now wavering halfway between them. "What about *his* life?" he said, pointing the gun again at Fedhisss.

Urr shook his head. "It would only result in the destruction of your town. If you want to save your town, then you must obviously shoot me. Now."

"Do it!" Fedhisss said, looking angry now. "Before I throw this lever and end your foolish hesitation."

Les looked at Anne, standing beside him, but he saw only his own pain and confusion reflected in her face. It was up to him to decide. He had to act before Fedhisss did. Swinging the gun back, and extending his arms again, he sighted down the barrel at Urr.

Urr remained calm as he watched Les closely. He appeared to be more interested in what would cause Les finally to act than in what was about to happen.

Les fought to keep the trade-off in mind, one alien life for all the lives in town. Was Fedhisss right, then? Why hesitate? Shoot! he told himself. Shoot, and be done with it! He could feel the frustration and the anger flooding through him as he tightened his finger again on the trigger, aiming now for the center of Urr's chest, as Urr stood quietly, waiting for the bullet to strike him.

"No!" Les cried out. "Damn it, no!" He swung the gun back to Fedhisss. "It's you, you sick-minded bastard! You're the one who deserves to die!"

"Touching," Fedhisss said. "Very touching. Don't you

think so, Urr? He simply cannot bring himself to shoot you. He would rather have me destroy his entire town. Oh, Urr. Look what you have brought him to." Fedhisss shook his head slowly. "But rather than have it come to that, I will make it easy for him. Look."

Les tensed as Fedhisss took hold of the metallic box sitting next to him.

"If you agree, Urr, I will tip my little device here and aim it down toward the ground in front of me. Then I will activate it enough to clear that area and anything that enters it. If you wish to save your young and foolish friend from the very rash act that he is about to commit, then I offer you the opportunity, with the same resulting terms, to choose to walk into that area with your own free will. Your young friend's conscience would then be clear, and I could depart this dismal planet. The decision is yours, Urr. You will now determine what happens next." Fedhisss turned away then, trying to appear disinterested, as though he were tired now of the whole game and it made no difference to him whatever Urr decided.

Urr nodded slowly. "Yes, Fedhisss, I accept your terms." He turned then to Les. "And I thank you for your kindness to me." He reached out and gripped Les's arm. "You and Miss Sommers. I am pleased to have made contact with you."

Urr stepped to the chain-linked fence and swung open the gate.

"Wait!" It was all happening too fast for Les. Moving to block Urr's way, he gestured, with a look of distaste, at Fedhisss sitting up on the beam. "You're going to turn that... thing loose on the rest of the universe?"

"What other choice do I have, Les? It's my responsibility. It will take me only a moment more, and then it will all be ended for you." He smiled sadly and entered the gate, heading toward the area on which Fedhisss was now focusing his device. The ground in the area was fizzling in different spots, with wisps of mist arising in place of the few weeds that had managed to root themselves there.

Fedhisss was now staring intensely at all of them, his face shining with a manic, distorting glee as he watched his carefully prepared plan about to fulfill itself with the shattering of Urr and the end of Urr's pursuit.

Les was barely aware then of what he did next. His welling anger, his sense of injustice, a swirl of different emotions twisted up through him. "No!" he cried out. "No!"

He lifted the gun again and gripped it firmly in both hands. Aiming as quickly and carefully as he could, he fired.

50.

Sitting up there on the beam, waiting excitedly for Urr to walk into the shattering area, Fedhisss made an easy target. But whatever rage had torn through Les, whatever had caused him to raise the gun with deadly intent, he had been unable to bring himself to shoot directly at Fedhisss. In a desperate attempt to save Urr, Les had aimed at the circular opening on the front of the device that Fedhisss was holding, hoping that he could damage it enough to shut it down.

He missed his target. It was too small a spot.

The bullet twanged as it hit the lower left corner on the front of the device, startling Fedhisss, who instinctively jerked his hands away. The impact of the bullet knocked down the front of the already tipped device and swiveled it towards his legs, still dangling there. The soft sound of a poof! was heard, and a cellular mist burst out of the bottoms of his pants legs.

Fedhisss screamed and fell over backwards. Trying to stop himself as he fell, he grabbed at the wires looping down from the rear of the device, caught hold, and jerked them from their connections. Fedhisss, the device, and the trailing wires came crashing down into a tangled heap just within the steel-beamed framework.

Les and Anne hurried through the gate and approached Urr, who was standing still as he considered the confusion that lay before him. "Such an interesting muddling of

thoughts and emotions. Apparently, he fell between the two."
He turned, looking somewhat puzzled, and sized up Les.
"You surprised me. I thought that once I had managed to
have him point his device away from your town, you would
shoot him. It was your best, perhaps your only, opportunity."

"Les is not a killer," Anne said. It was an unusual flash of
anger for her. "Stop trying to make him into one."

Les looked down at the gun he was holding, amazed that
he had actually fired it. When he saw Anne's troubled expression as she watched him, he clicked the safety on again
and slipped it back into his pocket.

Fedhisss lay unconscious on the ground within the steel-
beam framework. Urr made his way to him and bent over.
While touching the belt Fedhisss was wearing, Urr touched
the side of his own belt. Both belts glowed for a moment like
circles of swirling light and then dimmed out.

Les joined Urr to check on Fedhisss and saw the blood
pooling on the ground. Kneeling beside Fedhisss, he pulled
up the pants legs to see the damage. "Christ! Will you look
at that!" The left leg up to the middle of the calf and the
right foot were missing, leaving two cleanly cut stumps that
were welling blood. "If we don't stop that bleeding fast, he's
going to die, Urr."

Urr turned a puzzled look on Les. "You would try to
save him?"

"I'm not exactly crazy about the idea. But I can't just stand
here and let him die."

Urr was clearly impressed. "Neither can I, Les. We must
get him as quickly as possible to his vehicle. If we do not do
so in time, he will bleed to the point where his energy will
finally dissipate."

"Then let's try to stop the bleeding first." Les took a handkerchief from his pocket and rolled it up diagonally into a

tourniquet. "Anne, see if you can find a short, stubby stick outside the fence, something I can use to twist this. And here." He handed her the car keys. "There's a small length of rope in the trunk of the car. We'll need that, too." Les knelt down again beside Fedhisss and tied the tourniquet around his left thigh. Then he waited until Anne brought back the rope and a large stick. Breaking the stick in half, he slipped part of it under the handkerchief tourniquet and began twisting, increasing the pressure steadily until he was able to cut off the flow of blood in that leg. Then, as Anne held that tourniquet in place, he fashioned the rope into a second tourniquet, and with the remaining part of the stick, managed to stem the flow of blood in the second leg. With the trailing ends of the rope, he tied the two tourniquets in place.

"Urr, do you know where his vehicle is?"

"I do now." Urr touched his belt for confirmation.

"Then we'd better get going. Anne, you can drive. Urr and I will carry him into the back seat."

Les and Urr went to lift Fedhisss. But before doing so, Urr paused to examine the metallic box lying now on the ground. It appeared to be badly damaged by the fall, the top lid partially bent open and one side caved in. Urr reached in through the top and removed a small part. "It would be unwise to leave this behind." As he slipped it into a slot on the back of his belt, Les tried to look. "What is it?"

Urr straightened his belt again. "Something too irresistible for human nature. A power that would prove to be corrupting."

Les remembered the feeling of the gun in his hand.

Urr looked down at Fedhisss, who was still unconscious. "We'd better hurry now. If his containment expires, you will have a dead body on your hands to explain to your authorities."

Starting to bend over, Les jerked upright again. "Urr! What about the others? Professor Jurgens, and Bingo, and the student lab assistant?" He pointed at the distant woods. "And that path of destruction over there!" His voice was now frantic. "How am I going to explain them?"

Urr nodded. "You'll think of something."

Les thought a moment. "I will?"

51.

Following Urr's directions, Anne had driven back out to the dirt road east of town. As they drove past the area, Les recognized where he had parked the day before, when he had followed Urr into the woods to view his vehicle. They continued on for another half-mile. In the back seat, propped up between the two of them, Fedhisss had begun to stir, making low moans. "Here," Urr said. "You can pull off here."

Anne eased the car to a stop at the edge of the road, got out from behind the steering wheel, and opened one of the back doors, as Les and Urr struggled to lift Fedhisss out of the car. Climbing out, Les saw the two small pools of blood on the car floor where the stumps had rested. Two trickles of blood followed them as they got Fedhisss out. The tourniquets had not completely cut off the flow.

"Quickly," Urr said, as they carried Fedhisss between them into the woods, with Anne trailing behind. There was no clear path. Tree limbs and undergrowth scratched across them and pulled at their clothes, as though trying to prevent them from bringing such an undesirable visitor into their setting.

They had not gone very far from the road when they came into a secluded clearing, where they could see the small, ovoid vehicle, identical to the one that Urr had shown Les.

"His spaceship!" Anne said, remembering Les's words. Her eyes were wide with wonder as she moved slowly around the vehicle.

"Look inside," Les said, as he and Urr eased Fedhisss to the ground.

Anne went up and peered into the transparent dome, taking everything in, and surprised by the seeming simplicity of the interior. She turned back to Les. "It's so small inside. Barely enough room for one."

"One what?" Urr said, watching her now.

She considered his question a moment, and then smiled. "Of course. How foolish of me. I'd love to know what size you really are."

"And I, too, Miss Sommers, would like to know what size *you* really are, for you are clearly much larger than your physical nature."

"Less than a full day on earth," she said, "and you have already learned how to flatter women."

"Not flattery, Miss Sommers. That was a finding of fact."

"Get me out of here, Urr!" Fedhisss was fully conscious now, his face twisted with an agonizing pain. "Get me into my vehicle!" Reaching down, he touched his belt in various places, and then looked up at Urr with eyes burning with hatred. "Damn you! You compassionate fool! What have you done?" His voice still full of the excruciating pain, he shot a condemning look at Les and Anne. "A pathetically deficient life form...just beginning to leave its planet...should have been stepped on before it had the chance to spread." He appeared to be having trouble breathing. "And you... what have you done? Allowed them to persist. Not only as they are now...deplorable as that is. But for whatever they will become.... Unpredictable..... Their world...its mechanical workings...will continue to twist them into other...disruptive forms. Disorganizers...spreading out...in unending variations! Urr, you fool!"

Les glanced at Urr to see how he was taking it, and detected a trace of doubt passing like a shadow across his alien friend's features.

Fedhisss turned again with a menacing look to Les and Anne. "Maybe not." He tried to laugh, but the sound died in his throat. "Maybe not. All of you here...yes, I can see it... you will likely end up doing to yourselves...what I could have done...so much more efficiently. This planet...it doesn't deserve my presence. Get me out of here, Urr!" He shouted. "Get me out of—" His eyes froze in place, as though looking at something beyond sight, and then went blank. His head fell over to one side.

Les knelt quickly and felt for the vein at the side of his neck. "My God, Urr. His heart has stopped." He stood up with an anguished look.

"He's dead!"

52.

"QUICKLY, LES," URR SAID, as he started to lift Fedhisss. "Before it's too late. We must get him into his vehicle."

"Urr," Les said. still anguished. "Didn't you hear me? I told you he's dead."

"Not yet," Urr said. "His heart may have stopped, but he is not dead yet. We have a few minutes before that occurs. So hurry, Les. We must put him in the vehicle. In no time at all."

Moving quickly now, Les helped Urr to lift Fedhiss between them and start for the vehicle. As they approached it, to Les's surprise, a side section of the vehicle, like a ramp, swung down to the ground, and the transparent dome hinged up, giving them access to the interior. They struggled with their load up the ramp and, with difficulty, managed to get Fedhisss seated inside. With haste, Urr touched a series of places on what appeared to be a blank panel slanting toward the front of the seat. "Back now." Urr motioned to Les to go down the ramp, and then joined him on the ground beside the vehicle, where he took Les's arm and walked with him over to Anne, who had remained at the edge of the clearing. "Now," Urr said, watching the vehicle.

The ramp and the dome closed again, and the interior suddenly came alive with light. A steady glow mixed with muted pulsing flashes gave a pallid, eerie cast to the face they could see inside the dome. As though the vehicle were now dismantling, molecule by molecule, the containment that

Fedhisss had resided in, his face, like a pointilist painting, began to separate into a multitude of individual dots, which in turn began to separate into smaller dots, until the three of them watching could actually begin to see through Fedhisss.

Anne, caught by the sight of what was happening, reached out unawares for Les's hand and clutched it, unable to take her eyes from the dome as Fedhisss steadily disappeared before them.

They all glanced quickly down then as, beneath the vehicle, there was a sound of something metallic penetrating the ground. Into the loamy mixture containing the thousands of life forms that had emerged and roamed and crumbled back into the earth, the two probes had once again tapped into the organic leavings. But this time they were discharging the gathering of molecules selected earlier to construct a containment for the advanced level of organized energy known as Fedhisss.

Immediately after the probes were withdrawn, the lights within the transparent dome dimmed to a steady state, and the vehicle, rising slightly from the ground, paused, as though readying itself for something. And then, with a speed that caused Les and Anne, who were still holding hands, to stagger backwards together, it shot straight upwards into the sky, until, with a final distant glint from the late afternoon sun, it disappeared from sight.

Transfixed, Les still looked upwards, trying mentally to follow the vehicle as it moved beyond the protective atmosphere of earth into the unknown reaches of outer space.

"What will happen to him now?" Anne said, turning to Urr.

"He's being returned," Urr said.

"And then?" Les said. "What happens to him then?"

"The Circle will decide."

"The Circle," Les said, imagining some stern group of Urrs seated at a large, round table, frowning their displeasure.

"They will likely keep Fedhisss for a period of time in the state in which he is presently being maintained in his vehicle."

"Stored, you mean?" Les said.

"Ah," Urr said. "Your battery image again. Yes, something like that, but more organized."

"For how long?"

"Well beyond a good many of your millenia."

"But to what end?" Les persisted. "If he's simply stored the way he is, to be released at some later time, no matter how far into the future, what will be accomplished, except the delay? He will still be Fedhisss."

"True," Urr said. "But we will have gained additional knowledge by then, and perhaps by then we will know more decisively what we should do with Fedhisss"

"Perhaps," Les said, looking dubious. "Here on earth we would act to resolve the issue now. For the crimes he committed here, we would probably execute him."

"Yes." Urr nodded slowly and seriously. "I assumed you would, considering your natures and your circumstances. And I do not say that in a critical way. It is simply a recognition of where you are at this time, and, indeed, what you are compelled to do to maintain yourselves. But you are not a static species, Les. You will not always remain vulnerable to the mechanical workings of your world."

"What do you mean by that, Urr? What mechanical workings?"

Pausing a moment, Urr studied Les, as though considering the best way to answer. "Human beings have persistently placed their trust in things that happen *naturally*, for you believe that *natural* happenings are occurring as a part of some divine plan, and therefore must be *good*. After all, it has led, in the development of the universe, to your presence on Earth. This belief has been maintained through most of human history for the very simple reason that you recognized your helplessness in the face of that universe. The only choice offering you any psychic comfort was to accept the universe as *good*.

"But now you appear to be entering a new phase of existence, where your compounding knowledge is allowing you to consider choices that are better for humanity than natural occurrences. Think for a moment about what actually is *natural*, Les." Urr looked around the clearing they were in. "The same evolutionary process that has created human beings, and the blue beetle we saw on your kitchen floor, and the grass here on the ground around us, the same natural forces and materials that have brought forth the wide variety of life forms to be found here, is also creating albinos among you, and six-fingered hands, and mental retardation, and malignant tumors, and sterility, and heart defects. Naturally. You call these unwanted mutations *defects*. But they have been, and continue to be, a natural part of the evolution of life on earth. Why, then, do you remain so tentative about accepting responsibility for yourselves and your immediate world?"

He looked intently at each of them. "You must distinguish now in all of your activities between the mechanical processes of the evolving material universe, which have been going on since the beginning of time, and the influencing of those processes by a self-conscious being. By *you*, Les. And Miss Sommers. And many of your species. Your consciousness has now begun to emerge to a higher level. It will be of some interest to see what you do with yourselves."

There was a rustling among the leaves in the trees around the clearing. Glancing up at the sky, Urr enjoyed for a moment the feeling of a breeze on his face. The late afternoon light was beginning to wane.

"It's time for me to go."

53.

THEY RETURNED TO THE car, and Les drove them back to the area where Urr had landed his own vehicle. Entering the woods, Urr once again led them through the undergrowth, recalling for Les the ominous feeling that had come over him the night before as he had followed a stranger with increasing trepidation deeper into the darkness of the woods. They came again out into another clearing, where Urr stopped. "It will be best if you are not too close to my vehicle when I depart."

"But where is it?" Les said, looking around. He did not remember this open space.

"There in the woods, on the other side."

Crossing the clearing, they approached a less accessible area of more densely tangled tree limbs and undergrowth, where they were finally able to make out the vehicle, nestled just beyond the intervening leaves, almost out of sight. Anne smiled as she recognized its small, ovoid shape. "It looks like you do everything in twos. Are we going to see you disappear, too?"

Urr returned her smile. "Only for another millenium or two, Miss Sommers. But since the degree of my awareness also defines the extent of my responsibility, and since I am now aware of your planet, I will be returning in the future to see how you have progressed. I look forward to it, since I think you will do well."

She laughed lightly and took Les's arm. "In a millenium

or two, Les and I should be well stirred into the soil. Perhaps we could supply a few molecules for your next containment." Studying Urr a moment, she grew serious. "But there is a last question I would like to ask you. It's one that we have asked for as long as we have existed on this planet."

Urr nodded and smiled gently at her. "I understand, Miss Sommers, and my answer is no. A number of your religions have offered you, in good faith, if I may put it that way, the comforting thought of a personal afterlife. But I do not believe it."

"So we just die, and that's the end of it?"

"No," Urr said. "I don't believe that either."

"What, then?" Anne was watching him closely.

"Look there," Urr said, gesturing   across the clearing at a large maple tree that was towering above the woods. A soft, suffusing redness in the western sky was silhouetting the tree as the evening darkened.

"It's something like that tree," he said. "Think of life being like that tree, and each of you a leaf on that tree, emerging into this world as a living being and existing for a brief period of time before you wither up and die."

She frowned. "And that's the end of it?"

"Not really the end," he said. "Because the tree is never the same again. Every leaf adds something to the tree, however small, that is not lost when the leaf dies."

As she stood there quietly for a moment, he could see that she was troubled by his answer, still caught in a vague yearning for something more.

"Remember," he added, wanting to cheer her, "that if you consider the circumstances out of which you have emerged, it's remarkable that you have reached this point. And just think of the wealth of possibilities stretching out ahead of you." He gestured above him. "If you look straight up into that glimmering sky and try to see into the darkness that exists beyond the stars, you can imagine the earth being like some early sailing ship. You're on a voyage into unknown waters that were marked on your ancient maps, 'Here be dragons!' You're explorers on a wonderful adventure."

"Yes," she said, "on a ship without a captain, buffetted about by every passing wind." She smiled with effort. "Don't mind me. I always get a bit somber about this time of day."

"It's early days on your cosmic voyage," he said, still looking up. "You're only just beginning to take the helm."

"So what do we do in the meantime?" she asked, as the woods around them began to fill with darkness.

"In the meantime," he said, "you must keep a sharp eye out. And then, perhaps, you, too, at some future point will advance to where you will gain a clearer vision. But not," he added, "an ultimate vision."

Urr's expression had become bland again, but behind it, for a fleeting moment, she thought she had glimpsed the being who was within the body standing before her. It startled her, the intensity of its presence, widening her eyes. "I don't understand."

"Because," he said, "there is no ultimate vision. That is an unfortunate error that your species has insisted on committing, both within your sciences and your religions, across the entire span of your history. If I were to leave you and Les with a final thought, Miss Sommers, it would be this. Your currently held beliefs are dangerous if they encourage you to come to rest within them, and so leave you drifting with unconcern upon the still unplumbed depths of your ignorance. If you are ever to move beyond the tragic redundancies that characterize your natural lives, the killing and the suffering, the hunger and the cruelty, the multitude of other inflictions so often self-imposed, you must recognize that the responsibility for doing so is yours, and that you must be willing to take control of the helm on your voyage. If you are going to journey into realms that lie beyond the edges of your present awareness, you must avoid heading for the comforts of the nearest port, where you can drop anchor and leave the ship, as though you have arrived at some final destination. You will learn in time that your only destination has always been an endless journey."

He looked warmly at both of them. "I do like your metaphors."

Wait!" Les said, as a thought occurred to him. "Dr. Jurgens, and Bingo, and the lab assistant. How am I going to explain their disappearance?"

"They were gone before we arrived at the laboratory, Les. I would strongly recommend that you do not try to explain. What could you possibly say that would be seriously considered by your authorities? Let them be listed as missing persons. Your attempt to explain would be ridiculed and would, indeed, be considered a cruel hoax."

"And the woods?" Les said, still troubled. "The wide path of destruction through them. How do I explain that?"

Anne shook her head. "No one will think to ask you, Les. Dr. Urr is right. There is nothing we can say."

"But don't despair," Urr said, smiling. "Somebody will surely come up with the idea that the strange path through the woods was caused by aliens trying to send earthlings a message." He appeared to do a double-take. "And, you know, they will be right!" He laughed softly as he started into the woods at the edge of the clearing. A few feet in he turned and paused to look wistfully at each of them. "I am aware of how much you love each other, and of how love can have an unending influence beyond your lives. Your species will continue to strengthen its consciousness as it strives to extend its knowledge, and so I would encourage you to have your children and send them on into the future. It will indeed be at some cost, Miss Sommers. But eventually they will discover that they are not alone in their struggle to understand the nature and the workings of this universe. And they will also learn that they have a debt to the past, for I will be returning to tell them the story of how two harmless human beings managed to save their world."

He turned and went into the undergrowth to his vehicle. The woods were almost dark now. Through the screening leaves, they could barely see him mounting the ramp and entering the interior. Once again they could see the pulsing lights, but they were unable to make him out clearly. Once again, more faintly now, they heard the probes penetrating the ground. Standing there in the darkened clearing, they imagined Urr's containment being returned to the earth. And then, as before, with a startling speed, they saw the vehicle lift straight up into the evening sky, no more than the hint of a blurred point within their vision, before it disappeared into the darkness among the stars.

Without being aware of it, Les had put his arm around Anne. The two of them stood there in the clearing, still looking upward, reluctant to leave.

The breeze in the clearing was strengthening now out of the west, heralding a change in the weather. Sensing the approaching winds, Les held Anne closer as he recalled the voyage that Urr had earlier described for them. He could imagine that they were sailing now through the elemental forces that were spinning the earth they were standing on, whirling the planets around the sun, blowing them across their spiraling galaxy as it made its way among the other galaxies. They were heading outward on some fantastic journey toward someplace inconceivably distant, far beyond the scope of their present awareness, where something yet to be imagined would be waiting for them to arrive.

54.

BEFORE CONCLUDING MY REPORT, I note for the record that my initial response upon arriving on this planet was one of being drawn toward the perspective taken by Fedhisss, that there was a clear need to eradicate, without any hesitation, the wide variety of life forms existing here because they had been distorted into such vicious modes of survival by the inadequacies of their energy system. But my views were somewhat altered as I considered the progress made by the dominant inhabitants here. They are groping their way not only outward among the many forces and materials of the universe, among which they have been so fearfully awakened, but of greater significance and more immediate need, they are reaching inward, to touch and temper the still discordant movements of their own natures.

I have questioned if they are capable of breaking out of the self-centering world which they have so thoughtfully constructed around themselves. Do they have the ability to recognize that they are simply another part of this planet's erratically woven and often fraying fabric of evolving life forms? They have a deep, indeed a desperate, need to comfort themselves constantly with soothing assumptions, of a world unable to continue on without them, of the central role they must be playing within the workings of the universe at large. And yet they have managed in this way to fabricate for themselves, in the very midst of their maddening conditions, a somewhat sane and strangely proud existence.

Having spent my brief time here contained as one of the dominant inhabitants, I have exposed myself to their many vulnerabilities and the often irrational workings of their still indeterminate natures. A strange and deeply troublesome experience. Nevertheless, although clearly with some lingering confusion, I find myself departing this planet with the sense of wanting to cup my hands around it, as one would try to keep a flickering candle burning in the swirling wind, for the consciousness of their species can be seen now as the faintest of auras beginning to enlighten their world.

Will they be able to awaken further, and to accept responsibility for themselves, in time to outpace the uncontrolled universal forces yet to sweep across their fragile existence?

What the hell (I do like their jargon), it's up to them now. I'm out of here.